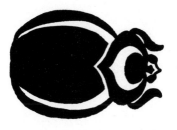

Treachery in Crete

Treachery in Crete

Written and Illustrated by

MYRON TIM PALMER

1 9 6 1

HOUGHTON MIFFLIN COMPANY BOSTON

The Riverside Press Cambridge

Also, by the same author,

The Egyptian Necklace

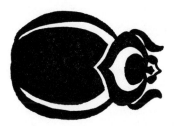

Treachery in Crete

AR, AND HIS FRIEND PTA sat under the tall sycamore tree in Ar's garden protecting themselves
from the scorching Egyptian sun. They were
whiling away their time, as restless as fifteen-year-
old boys can be, and wishing for something really
exciting to happen. Ever since they had played
such a large part in exposing the robbery of a
tomb, for which the Pharaoh had rewarded Ar
with a magnificent royal necklace, the boys had
found their ordinary life very dull indeed. Certainly they could not expect every day to afford
such events in quick succession. Nevertheless,
they hoped!

Yarem, the Phoenician, Ar's personal slave and
teacher, was almost as bored as the boys. He too
sat idly through the midday heat in the shade of
the sycamore, and he too was dreaming — dreaming of the day when he would surely be free

1

again. Slender and dark-haired, with coal-black eyes and a thin, high-arched nose, he had the look of breeding which clearly indicated that he had not been born a slave. He had grown up in Crete and upon reaching young manhood had been sent on a voyage concerning the family business enterprises — most young men of Crete took on adult responsibility early in life. There had been a shipwreck and he, the only survivor, was found lying exhausted on the northern shore of Africa. Promptly he was sold into slavery by the nomads who found him. In fact, he had been sold twice: once to an evil man employed by Het, the Pharaoh's architect, and then to Het himself. It was during his service to Het that he finally found an opportunity to explain to his master who he was, and he begged Het to send word to his people that he was alive and well. He was certain that his father would then buy his freedom. In the meantime Yarem was serving as tutor and companion to Ar, Het's son, and Pta, Ar's friend.

While Yarem mused upon his fate, the boys were mulling over the stories he had been telling them of his boyhood and the golden days when he had been free. In describing his family's great ships, Yarem had told how the wind blowing through the rigging made sounds like the music of a great harp, how the oarsmen rowed rhythmi-

Decoration of painted lilies and head of bull

cally to the beat of a red-bronze gong, and of the
strange and wonderful ports where they had put
in for trade. When he came to his encounter with
Scylla, the sea monster, dog and serpent com-
bined, the boys shuddered with horror and admired his courage. The sea, with its wide, dangerous reaches, fascinated them, although they had

3

no ability to appreciate its wind-swept freedom. They had never even seen the Deep Green, as the Mediterranean was called in those days.

Ar now remarked to Pta, "The last time I sat here and wished for something to do was the beginning of our adventure with the Queen's Necklace. How I do wish that something would happen now!" Pta agreed, whereupon Yarem said, "You two are wishing for adventure and I am longing for word from my family and my freedom. So perhaps we had better all wish to-gether — and wish hard."

At that moment, Ar's sister, Ahn, came racing into the sunlit garden, her clothing disarrayed, her face flushed with running. It was no way for the daughter of an important Egyptian family to behave, as the three who watched her knew. But, to add to their astonishment, she was closely pursued by Bu, the wrinkled, dignified major-domo of the House of Het.

She came up to them and stopped, a-quiver with excitement. Before she had time to say a word, however, Bu had joined the group under the sycamore. He motioned the girl to silence. He had an announcement to make, and no young girl was to be permitted to tell his news. "Young master!" he exclaimed, "Yarem! Come! My Lord Het summons you." But he could no longer sus-

4

tain his formality, so he added, "Never before have I seen the like of this. Come quickly and see for yourselves!"

The young men rose eagerly to their feet and followed Bu and Ahn while Bu continued exclaiming and muttering as he led the way through the bright sunlight to the main courtyard. Hurrying after him, Ar and Pta asked questions that were not answered, for Bu's chatter persisted unabated. He was too agitated to make sense. Yarem went right along with all of them but said nothing, as was fitting. He was the slave tutor.

In the courtyard the family of Het was assembled, and a stranger was talking earnestly with Ar's father. When Yarem drew near, he took one look at the stranger, gasped, and forgot he was a slave. Brushing past the boys so abruptly as to seem rude, he went straight to the stranger and exclaimed, "My uncle! At last, my uncle!" The scene was too touching for the family of Het to bear watching. With one accord, they tactfully looked the other way and talked quietly among themselves.

After this reunion, Het spoke to his Phoenician slave: "Yarem, I am delighted to learn that you have spoken truly to me of your family. I must confess that I needed proof that your people really were the family of Artish. All the world

5

knows of the great merchant family of the Isles of the Circuit. I am sorry that I doubted your word but, at any rate, it is all in the past now, and from this moment you are once again a free man. I congratulate you." Then he added, showing some embarrassment, "Your uncle has insisted upon presenting us with gifts." He indicated a line of sailors, standing in stiff formation along the court-yard, each with an open carved chest in his arms.

Yarem's uncle relieved the situation now by saying in faultless Egyptian, "It is but a small thing for us to do in return for tidings of my nephew. We feared he was lost to us forever. Now we can rest in our beds in peace, for we know that he lives to become the head of the House of Artish." He motioned the sailors for-ward and the gifts were formally presented to Het's family. Promptly everyone crowded round to see what was in the cases.

Only once before, at the reburial of the mummy of the Old Queen, had Ar seen such a wealth of beautiful objects. The first chests were packed to the top with folds of cloth, beautifully woven and dyed in yellows, reds, and violets, embroid-ered with strange and lovely designs of flowers and sea life. The next one contained carefully packed pottery; each piece was perfectly fash-ioned and decorated with designs which fitted

Egyptian receiving gifts from man of Crete

its form. But the third chest claimed Ar's whole
attention, and intrigued all the men present. It
was filled with bronze daggers inlaid with silver
and gold, double-edged swords the length of their
arms, and sharp javelin heads cunningly wrought

7

from the finest bronze. Ar gazed at this coffer in wonderment until an exclamation from his mother interrupted him. She was gazing with rapture into a chest containing many small colored boxes, overflowing with fragrant herbs and aromatic spices. These brought the perfumes of a strange world to the Egyptian courtyards.

Het offered formal but appreciative thanks for these royal gifts and then commanded that food and drink be brought for his visitors. As hosts and guests waited politely for the servants to bring in the tables of food, Ar and Pta stared openly at the sailors — they had never seen such costumes. These sailors were not Phoenicians, but men of Crete, small, dark men, bare to the waist except for their wide, finely wrought necklaces of carved stones. Broad waistbands held their knee-length skirts in place and pinched in their waists so tightly that the boys could not think how the men could breathe. These skirts were made of such fine material, so intricately woven and designed, that anyone could see that the sailors were dressed for no ordinary occasion. Their long, flowing hair was bound by rolls of cloth which matched their skirts. Ar and Pta, exchanging glances, had the same thought: how was it that these strangers did not know that

8

proper people shaved their heads and wore wigs?

Het had noticed the boys' curiosity with amusement and had not missed their little byplay. This was their first contact with the outer world. He spoke to them now while Yarem and his uncle chatted busily in their own language. "You will remember," Het told the boys, "that when I appointed Yarem your teacher he was supposed to teach you his own language and the ways of his people. I trust you have been good students, for now you should not be surprised at the dress of other lands. You will need your knowledge. I will tell you what we have had in mind all along for you if what Yarem told us about himself proved to be true; you are to go voyaging across the Deep Green. You will see and experience all that you have been preparing for these many months."

The boys stood large-eyed with excitement. They had never seen the Deep Green, let alone imagined floating across it to far lands. No one in Ar's family had so much as left the Valley of the Nile since the voyage of Ar's great-grandfather many years past. Ar leaped into the air for joy and turned to Pta to share his excitement. Pta was downcast and unhappy. "Why, Pta, aren't you glad?" he asked.

"You know, Ar, that there is no chance of my

going on such a trip. My father has not yet recovered from the adventure of the necklace and this will be too much, I know."

"You are wrong, my boy," Het corrected. "This plan has been discussed with your parents, and they are most willing for you to go. We have told you nothing about all this before because we had to await the outcome. But now I may tell you that you are both going." Then he added, "Ahn, stop pushing at me and wriggling. What is wrong with you?"

Ahn well knew how to make use of her ability to get attention. She continued to fidget and fuss. "I want to go too. Why should Ar go every place and I stay at home? It is not fair!"

Her father explained carefully that this was truly a voyage for boys only. There would be no place on board ship for girls. Ahn's interest abated as Het mentioned the hardships that she might be expected to share should she embark on such a trip. Ahn did not care for hardships. And when Ar promised to bring her presents she stopped pouting entirely and began to wonder what they would be like.

During the next two or three weeks she had many suggestions to make to her brother concerning the treasures that she hoped he would bring her from faraway lands. But Ar paid little attention. He was busy packing, unpacking, and repacking for the journey. He wanted to take just about everything he owned with him — fishing poles, fishhooks, bows and arrows, even toys that he was supposed to have outgrown. No one could dissuade him, or Pta either, for that matter. The boys compared notes daily and found they were having the same difficulties. While this was going on, Het and his distinguished guest were holding lengthy conferences.

The older Phoenician, it developed, was not returning to Crete at this time. Palaikastro, the home of his family, and of Yarem's, was a great port, but there were many other ports on the Deep Green, and almost all of them were home to some member of the Artish clan. Though Yarem's branch of the Artish family as well as his uncle's had made their homes in Crete, their native land was Phoenicia, that part of Asia lying at the eastern end of the Mediterranean. No matter where they lived, all the branches of this huge family proudly referred to themselves as Phoenicians. Het had hoped that Yarem's uncle would make the journey with the boys, but he had confidence in Yarem and knew that he would be a wonderful host and guide to them when they reached Crete. By now the boys had heard so much of the Land of the Keftiv from Yarem that

11

Map of the island of Crete

they imagined it to be a land of romance. Het remembered from his own youth how much even a short trip meant to boys just coming into manhood.

Yarem's uncle explained that he had come to Egypt with an empty ship. He had sailed in a great hurry when Het's message that Yarem was alive and safe reached him, Yarem's father being away at the time. Now cargo must be taken on in Egypt for exchange in Crete and he suggested that Het join him in the venture. Obviously, thought Het, this is a device of the Phoenician to show appreciation for our restoration of Yarem to his own people. Het felt badly enough to think that he had held so important a young man in slavery; he did not wish compensation for the loss

12

of a valuable slave. Finally, however, he had to
consent, so he suggested that Pta's father be included in the partnership. When all this had been
agreed upon, the shipment was planned. Gold
and copper would be desirable, Yarem's uncle
said, and dried vegetables, Egyptian spices, some
of the land's lovely blown-glass bottles and, for
ballast, fine hard basalt stone. His suggestions
were followed, a satisfactory cargo was assembled, and the day came when they were ready
to load the river boats. Then the uncle had another idea — he proposed that Ar and Pta journey to Crete as official representatives of their
families' interests, with Yarem to act as their
adviser. Thus they would acquire actual business
experience along with the pleasures of travel.
The result was that Ar and Pta strutted just a
little when they embarked on the river boat for
the trip on the Nile.

Het, beaming with pleasure, came hurrying
down toward the now loaded river boat. He
carried a covered reed basket. Ar looked at him
in amazement. It was most unusual for his father
to carry any sort of package; that was the duty
of his slaves. Once Het reached the party at the
dock, he began speaking: "Yarem, I have succeeded in getting permission from the high priest
Wah to give to your family one of Egypt's most

precious gifts. Ar has here for your mother a pair of the sacred kittens. Also a papyrus giving you permission to take them to your own land without fear of the death penalty."

Yarem looked pleased but his uncle seemed amazed. Yarem explained, "The cat is sacred to the Egyptian and there is a serious penalty for even hurting a cat. To send one from the country is a death offense. Furthermore, they are the best protectors against rats and mice about the granaries. Thus it is, my uncle, we are being given one of the highest honors possible for an Egyptian to pay."

Both Yarem and his uncle made the proper formal thanks for the gift and turned to board one of the cargo boats that would take them all from Thebes to the mouth of the Nile River.

The boys put on a brave front at departure but Ahn made a big to-do about what Ar was to bring her from the Isles of the Circuit. Even when seeing them off, she felt that it was necessary to remind Ar of his promise. He paid little or no attention, for he was used to Ahn's insistence. All she wanted, he thought, was to be the center of attention. He told her that if she did not stop coaxing at once, he would bring her none of the presents she had requested. That silenced her. Yarem, remembering also some of Ahn's previous performances, smiled with amusement as he listened to the exchange between brother and sister.

The boys waved farewell as long as they could make out the faces of their families, then settled in for the trip down river to the Delta of the Nile. For the first stage of the journey they were on a river boat, one of several carrying their cargo to be transferred to the large Phoenician ship later. The villages and papyri beds that they passed were just like the villages and papyrus beds they knew at home. When they reached the Delta

Sea-going ship

everything changed. The boys could see nothing but ships — ships of every size and variety, coming and going ceaselessly. The town given to the Cretan traders by the Pharaoh and the docks of the people of Crete bustled with activity.

All along the shore and out onto the docks men carried bales, chests, bundles, rolls of cloth, baskets of foodstuffs . . . Yarem observed the boys with amusement; for once they were too busy watching what went on to ask questions! He joined them at the side of the boat and identified the strange ships, pointing out people from other lands who traded through the Isles of the Circuit. As they drew near to the unloading dock, Ar pointed at a man in astonishment. "How strange he looks!"

"He is one of our men," Yarem remarked. "He comes from the mainland to the north which is called Mycenae." Then he called, "Ho, Lysis!" The man turned and now the boys could see his white skin, golden hair, and blue eyes. They gasped in wonder. Everyone in the world they knew had black eyes!

"Is he sick? Or is he a freak like those who perform in the market place?" asked Ar.

"He is neither. He comes from the north where most of the people are of the same coloring. Just wait until you see the first one with hair the color

16

of fiery gold, like a flame. Then you will be surprised."

It was time to go ashore and to take their leave of Yarem's uncle, who planned to sail as soon as possible on another of the Artish ships bound for Tiryns.

In the bustle of landing Ar had forgotten the strange, fair man until he turned up at Yarem's elbow, waiting to speak to him. With him was a Negro and, standing side by side, the two looked like twin statues of ebony and ivory.

"Ubi!" exclaimed Yarem, recognizing the Nubian, who like Lysis was his personal servant. Yarem introduced them to the boys, and then led the way toward the town. Through a busy section of shops and storehouses they advanced, Yarem explaining over his shoulder that he was taking them to the house of his cousin Hatich, who his uncle said was stationed here. They passed booths selling rope, heavy brightly colored cloth for sails, tools, food — all in such confusion that it seemed as though no one could ever sort out the merchandise, let alone sell it. Proceeding through the crowds in single file, Pta had somehow dropped behind.

When Ar turned to speak to him, he was just in time to see Pta pulled into a stall where sailcloth was sold. Pta was fighting and squirming

17

desperately, but he could not call for help because a brawny sailor had clapped his hand over Pta's mouth. There was nothing wrong with Ar's mouth, however, and he instantly let out such a shout that it sounded shrilly above all the clamor of the market place. Yarem spun around in time to see the whole situation at a glance. He yelled in his turn, high-pitched and piercingly, "Artish! Artish!"

With that the whole market exploded into action. Yarem's cry was picked up and echoed, a flurry of fighting broke out, and the sailor who had seized Pta quickly let him go, disappearing into the shop behind them. Yarem reached Pta at once and simultaneously, a group of sailors moved up beside him, indicating clearly that they were there as guards.

"Pta, what on earth happened?" asked Ar. "Did you do anything to start all this?"

"No," gasped Pta, "all I did was to stop at that shop there. Oh, I leaned down to look inside. I wanted to see what else they had. Then that old sailor reached out and grabbed me. There were two or three others there, sailors too, and a man who was dressed like the men of Crete. He wore a gold armlet set with a bright, shiny red stone, but I could not see much of him. I didn't say or do a thing! I am the one who wants to know what happened!"

Pta was looking at Yarem as though he expected him to have the answer, which increased Yarem's discomfort. This was a poor start for Yarem as protector of his guests. He listened gravely as Pta tried again to tell what had happened, but he could offer the boys no explanation. By the time they reached the house of Yarem's cousin, they had fairly exhausted the subject until Ar remembered one more question. "Why," he asked Yarem, "did you shout your family name in the market place?"

"For help," Yarem replied. "There are men of my family, or attached to my family, in just about every port on the Deep Green." He had raised the rallying cry because he wanted help — and he got it. Had not the boys seen the guard of sailors who appeared so silently and so suddenly?

As he spoke, they entered the lower part of a house. There they were met by Hatich, Yarem's cousin, who had been destined to be the head of the House of Artish if Yarem did not return.

Hatich was a small, dark, slender young man, somewhat older than Yarem, of more than average good looks. His greeting to Yarem was friendly enough, but he failed to congratulate

19

him upon his return from the Land of the Shades and his release from slavery. To the boys he was coldly formal. This disturbed them. Was not this house really Yarem's property? And should not Hatich be polite to Yarem's guests? They in turn became as formal as they knew how to be. Never let it be said that Egyptians did not know their manners. Pta, however, lapsed a little in courtesy, for he was staring intently now at Hatich. When Ar noticed this and asked him what was wrong, Pta merely shook his head in a puzzled way.

The next few days passed in a rush of arrangements. The gaily painted river boats were unloaded. Yarem, roll of papyrus in hand, checked everything brought from the boats with the list of articles written upon it. The boys wondered how he could read what he wrote, for he was not using the picture writing with curved lines that he had used in Het's house. He was writing with short, straight strokes that meant nothing to the boys. Then he personally sealed each chest and bale with red wax, rolling a small seal of carved stone through the hot wax, thus leaving its impression. The boys watched the process carefully. They had to, they knew, for were they not the representatives of their families? At last the day of departure arrived.

Carved seals of Crete

A good breeze blowing from the hot south would carry them northward. The trading ship of the Phoenicians, in which the goods had been duly loaded, was the largest they had ever seen. They had explored it at intervals when they had a chance. They knew that it was round-bottomed and broad in the middle and that its stern and bow rose to equal heights. The heavy polished bronze ram, or beak, attached low on the bow, glittered in the sunlight. There was a deck over the banks of rowing benches and the sails and rigging almost brushed it. The sail could be used, of course, only when the winds favored them; at other times they would be furled and the oarsmen set to rowing. Two men manned the two rudders, which looked like oversized oars and were painted with great staring magic eyes in order to help guide the way. Just as they were about to sail, the morning sun painted everything in glowing colors and even the dirt and dust of the port looked like dancing flecks of gold. The ship floated gently away from the dock. The hired oarsmen began rowing to the rhythmic beat of the bronze gong.

It seemed to Ar and Pta as though they were standing still but the town was floating away from them. Watching it gradually grow smaller, they found the sight entrancing. When finally they turned forward, there was nothing but the Deep Green. Looking backward again, no land was in sight. At once each boy felt a bottomless pit in his stomach, and they moved closer together. Yarem had been afraid of this, so he quickly stepped between them, putting his arms across their shoulders. He began to speak of all the fine things they would be seeing in a few days. The ship was perfectly safe, he said casually, because all the proper sacrifices had been made and there was even an altar to the god of the Sea on the ship's bow. Furthermore, the magicians and priests he had consulted in port had looked into the future and reported that all would go well with this voyage.

The ship bobbed and rolled gently in the clear sunlight. Suddenly, Ar discovered that there was a bottom to his stomach after all. He looked at Pta, who was gazing straight ahead, his eyes glassy, his color strange and grayish. Ar thought that his friend looked just the way he felt. Then both lunged for the side of the ship. For the next hour both boys were convinced that all magicians were liars and fakes and that they were about to die horrible deaths. By evening, though weak, they both felt somewhat better and found no difficulty sleeping on the rolling deck.

By morning they were sure that life was worth living. They found their appetites again, for one thing. The warm south wind blew steadily and the ship no longer felt like one of their own spinning tops bouncing over a rough floor.

Most of the day passed pleasantly until late in the afternoon, when there was a stir throughout the ship. The cause of the commotion was two ships in the distance. This was more like it. The boys had become rather bored with nothing but the unchanging sea to look at. Yarem, however, was studying the ships carefully and murmuring to himself. Perhaps . . . well, maybe . . . but . . . The boys watched him attentively, wondering. Then the captain, who stood nearby, caught Yarem's glance and nodded to him. Something was going to happen — something of importance evidently. Suddenly the captain turned and began to bellow orders so rapidly that the boys had to give up trying to translate what he was shouting. The bronze gong began to sound, faster and faster, oars were thrust out — sailors rushed on deck from all parts of the ship. They carried javelins and shields of a strange shape unlike those of Egypt. Then others ran forward bearing bows and arrows. Slowly the ship changed its course to take greater advantage of the wind. The oarsmen bent to their task to the sound of the gong, the ship began to gather speed, but the distance between it and the two smaller ships continued to lessen rapidly.

Yarem dashed off and came back almost at once with his arms full of shields and weapons. He was followed by Lysis and Ubi, who proceeded to fasten shields to the boys' left arms, indicating that they might have their choice of bows and arrows or spears. While this went on, Yarem walked quickly along the lines of sailors whose shields formed a wall along the whole length of the ship. They were ready. Returning to Ar and Pta, Yarem said just one word: "Pirates!"

"What are pirates?" asked Ar. Yarem looked at him blankly. Did not the boy know about pirates? Then he remembered that this was the first time they had ever been at sea. He explained quickly that just as there were sometimes robbers on roads ashore, so there were sometimes robbers at sea. These were called pirates. He turned to look at his forces; the armed men were evenly divided on each side of the ship, waiting and watching. Their hands rested on the swords and daggers that hung at their waists, or held javelins or bows and arrows. Lysis and Ubi stood on either side of Yarem, who now placed Ar and Pta between each of them and himself. The boys clung sturdily to their weapons and were glad that they had practiced with javelins and bows and arrows at home. They held their shields as the others did and they, too, waited.

The pirate ships had drawn closer, and now they could see the men on board. Clearly they were preparing to attack. The two smaller ships came along each side of the slower heavier vessel and suddenly a shower of arrows clattered to the deck. Others bounced off the shields of tough cowhide. Ar felt a thud on his shield and realized that an arrow had scored a direct hit. "Keep your shields up!" Yarem urged, "but do not use your weapons until I tell you to." The boys did as they were told, but the waiting was about the hardest thing they could ever remember having to do. On the enemy ships they could see men moving about in what appeared to be perfect safety. They were busy coiling long, heavy ropes into loose piles, and the boys noticed that each of these ropes had a kind of metal claw attached at one end. No one on Yarem's ship shot a single arrow to interfere with them or to defend himself. The Phoenician and Cretan sailors simply stood and waited for orders. It was very odd, the boys thought. Even a token flight of arrows would help . . . why was Yarem waiting? What for? Then, abruptly, the captain snapped an order. The boys stiffened. This was it, their first battle. The ship gave a great lurch and Ar lost his balance and almost fell. Swinging about, the heavy ship headed straight toward one of the nearby smaller ships. There was sudden panic and commotion as the pirates struggled to turn their ship in the same direction and get out of the way. A shower of arrows fell on the Phoenicians' deck; the second pirate ship was trying to aid its companion. Two or three of Yarem's men fell; watching the maneuvers they had forgotten to shield themselves. Their bodies were pulled back from the line in a manner that seemed dreadfully casual to Ar. Just then, Pta, who had not taken his eyes from the bronze beak at their ship's bow, shouted jubilantly. The shudder of a collision ran through the whole ship. The beak had reached its mark in the stern of the pirate ship and had in the process snapped off its great rudder oars like twigs. The steersmen were catapulted into the

A young man of Crete brings an offering to
the priestess. The feeling of movement in
the naturalistic patterns of the fish, flowers
and octopus are characteristic of the art
of Crete.

sea. The Phoenician captain had hoped to inflict greater damage but Yarem, watching, called, "Let fly!" and arrows poured into the crippled enemy ship. They could see the pirates drop in their lines; a noticeable toll was being taken. Throughout the confusion both parties were screaming wild threats and loosing arrows as fast as possible.

Then from the other side of the Phoenician vessel, came the sound of wood splintering, yells of rage and screams of pain. The captain quickly directed his ship to be turned in a great reverse circle. Yarem yelled to his men to keep up the fight on this side and motioned to his four to follow him. They rushed across the deck. There Ar could see that the pirates had succeeded in grappling the rails with their bronze claws, and while some pirates pulled on the attached ropes to keep the ships closely engaged, others were coming aboard. The Phoenicians were defending their ship heroically, hacking the ropes with swords and thrusting at the pirates with short, swift jabs of their javelins. Still, pirates swarmed up the ropes, and whenever one pirate fell, two seemed to take his place. It was horrible to watch those savage white faces appear at the ship's side and, at the sight, Ar suddenly howled with rage and called on all the gods of Egypt for help. So intent was he on the battle that when an arrow whizzed past his shield and struck between his chest and arm, nicking away a sizable piece of his skin, he hardly noticed it. His fury at the invaders was too great. By this time some of the pirates had gained a foothold on deck and fierce hand-to-hand fighting had broken out. The entire ship was filled with screaming, thrusting, and counterthrusting confusion.

Ubi appeared beside Ar, grunting and groaning under the weight of a huge piece of the heavy basalt stone that had been brought along for ballast. Yarem had been waiting for this and now with a glance and a short word to Ar the two of them stepped forward, using their shields to protect Ubi. Slowly, his muscles rippling and straining, Ubi raised the great stone above his head, using every ounce of his giant strength. At that moment, Yarem nodded to Ar; they stepped back, leaving Ubi unprotected for the second it required to heave the rock into the enemy ship. It landed first on the yielding bodies of pirates who screamed in terror and then crashed through the flimsy deck into the ship's waist, from which more shrieks resounded. The pirate ship was a shambles now, they hurriedly cut themselves loose from their grappling hooks and tried to get away from the big ship; those still on board her dived into the sea. The stone had gone straight through the deck and on through the bottom of their ship and, as far as they were concerned, the battle was over. The sudden silence was one of the most awesome things Ar had ever experienced. He turned to Pta.

Pta was lying unmoving on the deck behind him. Shaken with fear for his friend, Ar quickly knelt beside him. At the same moment Yarem dropped to the deck and kneeling at the boy's side, he felt over Pta's body gently. Then he looked at Ar and smiled. Ar was outraged. There was nothing to smile about with Pta senseless before them! "Pta is all right," Yarem said. "He is all right, Ar. He has taken a nasty crack on the head, that is all. He will come to soon with a sore head and the chance to wear an honorable scar." Ar sat down on the deck with a thud, he was so relieved. "You are going to bear an honorable scar yourself," said Yarem. "Look at your side." It was the first time Ar had become aware of his wound.

All over the ship the sailors were busily storing arms and shields, clearing the debris from the deck. They carefully unhooked the bronze claws in order to save the valuable metal. They bandaged wounds as they discussed their valor and bravery. Everyone on board the Phoenician ship considered that they had come out of the encounter well, with one ship rammed and greatly damaged and the other doubtless going to the bottom. They did not even look toward the scene of the battle to see what had become of the pirates' ships.

Gradually Pta recovered and as he and Ar walked among the men, they were greeted with smiles and accepted as part of the crew. The boys had given their life blood and come through the ordeal like men.

Dolphins swam and played along each side of the ship while gulls dipped and floated overhead. Yarem and the captain, however, were still talking about the attack. "I don't understand it at all," said the captain. "The Royal Navy of Crete

Dolphin and octopus

has kept the pirates down for years. Yet the boldness of these villains today reminds me of the old times when they roamed unchecked. It is odd. Furthermore, I have a feeling that these ships were following us. I cannot think that it was merely a chance encounter. It was by design." Yarem agreed with him. It had been strange. There was nothing more to fear, though. He could use some rest, he said. He was going to bed and Ar and Pta were willing to go also. Pta still had a headache.

The night passed uneventfully. Morning found the wind still favorable and their ship moved across the water like a bird skimming the waves. Ar and Pta had their sea legs by now and were really beginning to enjoy life at sea. In midmorning of the fourth day, a cry was raised and looking toward the horizon they could see a faint irregular line of mountainous land emerge against the sky. It was Crete. They had sailed too far west on their northwest voyage and now they turned east-northeast. Sailing along the coast, the ship neared a point of pink mountainous land rising from the deep blue sea. There the boys could see, marching up the mountainside, the large, spreading city that was called Palaikastro. Yarem, after his first long, eager look at his home, fell silent. He had wondered so often whether he would see it again!

Ar and Pta moved away and left him alone with his thoughts.

Palaikastro looked charming. The sunlight picked out all the pinks, blues, yellows, and reds in the town — the painted and decorated houses, even the tinted sails in the harbor. Little boats were being rowed out from shore to the incoming ship. One, larger and gaily painted, was obviously a pleasure craft. When Yarem saw it, he leaned far out over the railing. A woman was waving to him from the bow. Yarem began to wave wildly, and finally, unable to contain himself any longer, he launched himself with a high, arching dive into the sea and joined the playful dolphins. He swam straight for the boat.

Immediately a small rope ladder was flung over the side of the little boat. Yarem swam strongly toward it, gained the deck, and rushed, dripping wet, to the woman who waited.

"That must be his mother," said Ar.

"She won't mind that he is wet," said Pta thoughtfully, "because she thought he was dead and now she has him back again." Ar nodded. "Did you ever see a woman dressed like that?"

Pta never had. Yarem's mother wore many skirts of different shades of violet, one on top of the other, each one a little shorter than the one below it with the result that they flared out all

round her. The jewels that edged her brief, low-
cut jacket glinted in the sunset, flashing rainbow
colors. All this was strangely beautiful, but the
way she wore her hair was oddest of all. It was
arranged carefully in flat curls that went right
across her forehead in the manner of bangs; there

Mother Goddess of Crete, and Isis, the Mother Goddess of Egypt

were twin ringlets in front of each bejeweled ear, and the rest of her hair waved softly to her shoulders, held in place only by a ribbon. It seemed to the boys a very peculiar way for a mother to wear her hair. They wondered what Yarem's mother could be like.

Their captain led them to the side of the ship and directed them down a swaying rope ladder into one of the small boats which had come out to meet them. Ar, before leaving the big ship, had hurried to fetch the basket of kittens which he carried with great care. He knew that Yarem would understand why he had brought them along even though Yarem had seemed to forget them. Sacred cats were not to be forgotten! Yarem was waiting on the deck of the small pleasure boat to introduce Ar and Pta to his mother. The boys found her charming and very pretty. Yarem reached out for the basket with the kittens, rapidly explaining to her what was in it and what was meant by such a gift. She peered into the basket at the cuddly baby cats and exclaimed over them. The boys looked pleased but at the same time they were aware that few people could resist the sight of small playful kittens and they wondered if she really understood their true value. They came to the landing and all stepped ashore, Yarem now carrying the basket. This was proper respect and the boys appreciated it.

They had taken but a few wobbling steps when they concluded that the land of Crete was unlike anything they had expected. The people wore strange clothes, spoke a strange language, and the earth itself moved, its rhythm the same as that of the waves of the sea! But the people here were strangest of all for they could keep their balance even though their land swayed underfoot. How did they do it, Ar asked Pta. Pta thought it must just be that they were used to it.

Mother Artish could understand the Egyptian language, and as she watched the boys' unsteady gait and listened to their curious remarks, she was amazed. The earth on Crete never moved — unless there was an earthquake. What was the matter with these boys? Yarem had been chuckling to himself over their actions but now, seeing his mother's puzzlement, he laughed outright. The boys were all right, he told her. It was simply a case of sea legs with them. They had never been to sea before. His mother laughed also and then told the boys that the earth of Crete was steady enough — it was just that their own legs were not. "You must now find your land legs," she said.

The boys, much relieved, found each step easier than the last. They were on a road unlike any they had ever seen before. Since it climbed the mountain, it was a stairway of long, shallow steps that made the ascent easier. At one place a bronze lion head was fastened to a wall; water gushed from its mouth into a basin where it drained away out of sight. This astonished them. Imagine precious water being permitted to flow away, for all the world as though there would never be a shortage! Yarem pushed them gently forward and a few more steps brought them to a long high blank wall, which must, they decided, be the front of the house itself. There was an entrance near the corner of the building, not in the center of the wall where all proper Egyptian doors were situated.

Once in front of the door, Mother Artish turned to the boys and welcomed them formally to the house. Servants waited inside with lighted torches, which burned steadily, giving off sweet-scented smoke. They entered a large room rather than a garden as in Egypt, which was clearly not designed as living quarters; it seemed intended for storage. They had noticed when they came in how heavy and thick were the outside walls. Now they saw, stored against them, huge bins and tiers of shelves that were filled with chests. The chests were sealed with colored wax bearing the Artish imprint. There were great jars of baked clay standing about, taller than a man. The boys wondered what they held. The servants lead them past the jars to a staircase that went apparently to a blank wall. When they reached this wall, the stairway turned to go around it at a landing and then it mounted higher. At home in Egypt the stairways went straight from one place to another, they did not turn.

"Our house," Yarem explained, "was built to be used as a fortress should the need arise. Fortunately, it never has; but, it is easier to guard a stairway that turns, easier to guard and defend. You will notice that the stairs always turn to the right. An attacker on these stairs would thus be exposed since he would carry his shield on his left arm."

Now they came to the living quarters of the house, and when the door was opened, they stepped into a new world. They had grown up with painted walls and were used to considerable color in the home, but they had never imagined anything like this! All around the walls, painted flowers delicately swayed in the breeze and slender men and women marched in never ending procession. There seemed to be so much movement that the boys were almost sure that pipers who led a procession of painted figures were beating time with their heads and arms. Dolphins swam in a painted sea on another wall, freely, without the stiff formality of Egypt. The open windows facing toward a terrace were hung with woven draperies that swayed a little in the breeze — all was light and movement in the room! The floors were strewn with animal skins. Here and there about the room beautiful braziers of bronze threw out perfumed waves of languid smoke that threaded the area with a delightful pattern of color and light. Yarem must be a young Pharaoh in Crete to live in such a palace! Ar and Pta were overwhelmed by all this beauty.

Mother Artish clapped her hands and servants came in from another corner door which the boys had not noticed. The small table they carried between them was loaded with dishes — many kinds of foods in strange, new sauces, delicate wheaten cakes, honey, a wide variety of fruits, and wine. So much of the food was unknown to the boys that they were not sure how it should be eaten. They waited politely to see how Yarem would do it. When he took a cup of wine and poured a few drops on the tiled floor, they did the same thing. Mother Artish looked pleased at this, but the boys had no idea what the ceremony implied. Afterward they were to learn that it was offered in libation or prayer to the Great Mother Goddess of Crete. Following Yarem's lead, the boys ate and found that they enjoyed the food. Yarem and his mother talked together quietly at intervals. When the boys had finished, they were told of the plans for them.

Mother Artish said that since the boys were in an unfamiliar land they might like to share a bedroom. She did not want them to feel lonely in Crete. Ar and Pta thanked her and said they would like this. Then Yarem led them to their room in the men's quarters, stopping on the way to point out their bath, consisting of a stone basin sunk into the floor. Here they found running water, both hot and cold. This, to them, was another wonder. In their room they found soft beds and woolen blankets. They had realized even now before it was quite dark that Crete's night air was cold, compared with Egypt's, and the blankets were welcome. They took quick baths with none of the bathing ritual they were accustomed to in Egypt and were soon in bed. Before sleep came to them, they talked of what they had seen, deciding that they would let their hair grow and try to wear the clothing of the island people. Unless they did so, they agreed, they would feel strange. "Who wants to be odd?" said Pta dreamily as he drifted off to sleep.

Servingmen awakened them next morning. The boys found that Yarem had foreseen that they would wish to dress as his people did, so he had sent new clothing to them. Ar and Pta dressed as quickly as the unaccustomed garments permitted, with a few remarks about one another's novel appearance, after which they followed a servant to the roof that formed a terrace, shaded by vines and flowering shrubs. Here they joined Yarem and his mother to eat breakfast of fruits, melons, and cakes. They were just finishing when they heard a high clear call from within the house, and a girl came to stand in the doorway. Her skin was a pale gold and her black curly hair fell to her shoulders. She was pretty, the boys supposed. Yarem rose at once to bow and the boys copied him. The girl came to the table. She was about fifteen, Ar thought, slender and graceful. Mother Artish put an arm around her and introduced her to the boys. She was Nari, daughter of the high priestess of the Great Mother Goddess. Nari was casual about meeting the boys from Egypt; judging by her behavior, they might have lived next door! But she displayed considerable interest about what games they played and the sports of Egypt. Soon all three were chatting happily together. Yarem interrupted only when he felt a bit of translation would help out.

"Women," Yarem lost little time in telling Ar and Pta, "have a much more important position in Crete than in Egypt." Ar was inclined to agree, for he had never talked so much to a girl, apart from his sister, in his life. It would not have been seemly in Egypt. Perhaps Nari sensed this: at any rate, she now turned to address Yarem. She would give the visitors a rest.

"I was surprised to see your cousin Hatich as I came through the market place. What is he doing here?"

"You must be mistaken," Yarem replied. "We saw him in Egypt and left him there when we sailed. He could not have come on a later ship than ours because we just arrived last night. And certainly we did not bring him. You mistook someone else for him."

"No, I do not think I did," said Nari, "for I thought he recognized me. In fact, when he saw me coming, he streaked into one of the shops, and when I came up to it, he was nowhere to be seen."

"Oh, it cannot have been Hatich," said Mother Artish, "for he has not yet been given permission to come back to the Island. Of course, Yarem, he is something of a headlong fool, we know . . . Last year, after being informed that there were pirates between here and the mainland, he sent a ship out just the same without an escort. The result was that the ship has never been heard from since. It was a total loss and there was no excuse for it. It was poor judgment, to say the least."

41

She and her son promptly engaged in a discussion of family affairs. The boys sat quietly by. Nari took this opportunity to study them; they were something new.

After a while she asked them if they would like to go swimming. Ar and Pta did not know what to say. At their hesitation Nari turned to Yarem and asked, "Can it be that these boys do not know how to swim?"

"Swimming is looked on with disfavor in Egypt," Yarem informed her. "It is not safe because of the crocodiles in the Nile."

"Whatever are crocodiles?" Nari asked. And when Yarem finished his description, she remarked that it must be the Egyptian river's Scylla or witch.

Feeling discredited, somehow, Ar hastened to inform Nari that wrestling was really his sport. Nari looked delighted. "Fine!" she said. "We will all go swimming. Yarem and I will teach you. After that I will wrestle with you." The boys were horrified and amazed at the idea of a girl wrestling. They did not know what to say. Yarem came to their rescue, explaining, "I have already pointed out that the life of women in Crete differs from that of women in Egypt. It is greatly different, as you will discover. Wrestling is in no way unusual among the women here. Also, you must

42

have observed that my mother runs the business while my father is absent. For your own pleasure, you should learn to swim right away, for we go down to the shore nearly every day for fun and sport."

In the afternoon they left the terrace and went down through the storage room, pausing this time to measure themselves beside the tall jars which towered above them. Today the boys noticed that bands of raised clay, straight and wavy ran around the shoulders of the jars. They seemed too beautiful to be used for the mere storage of foods. It seemed that everything in Crete was decorated. This was not unusual to the boys but the type of decoration was quite different from Egypt's. In Egypt each unit of the design stood by itself but here one unit flowed into another, giving graceful movement. In any event, this characteristic in painting, and pottery alike, interested the boys who were used to the more formal static design of their homeland.

Emerging into the sunlight, the boys looked down over the harbor. The buildings stepped downhill, one after another, their brightly painted plastered walls aglow in the shimmering light. Their supporting painted beams exposed on their surfaces added a feeling of strength as well as beauty to the whole. Many buildings were two and three stories high and seemed higher because of being on the mountainside. Yarem waited as the boys admired the unfamiliar scene; then he said, "As long as it is on our way and while we are at it, we may as well stop and order seals for you. This will be necessary since you are the business representatives of your families. A seal is the only signature that is accepted by everyone here."

They had seen Yarem use his seal in Egypt and the idea interested and pleased them. Nari, watching Ar and Pta, thought that theirs must be a strange land indeed! The people did not use seals for business; boys could not swim — and all upper-class Egyptians shaved their heads! The four of them went on down the endless steps to the shops. Entering one, they found themselves in a lapidarist's workroom where stones were being cut and polished. "Wouldn't it be nice for the boys to have seals showing the Great Mother?" Nari suggested to Yarem. "She would protect them as strangers in the land. They could also add a symbol to represent their own country. Perhaps a lotus flower, such as the Egyptian painter drew for my mother's room."

Yarem turned to the boys, who agreed. Eagerly, they all examined the precious stones that awaited carving. There were pieces of clear crystal, agate, red carnelian — so many stones in such variety that Ar and Pta found themselves confused at having to make a choice.

"Will you choose for me?" Ar asked Nari. "I know nothing about all this and there are such a lot of stones!"

Pta asked Nari to choose for him too and, with that off their minds, the boys moved closer to watch Ish, the gem carver. They could tell from the respect with which Yarem and Nari addressed the old man that he was important in the city. Obviously, such men with their seals would be the guardians of all business and trade — of honest business and trade, at least. Nari, after a little indecision between two or three stones, now picked a purple amethyst for Ar and a red carnelian for Pta. She explained to Ish that Ar should have a fruitful palm tree, symbol of the Goddess, with a lotus at one side; and Pta a small scene of the sacrifice of fruits and flowers. They would both have much the same meaning. Ish accepted the idea and made quick sketches with charcoal on a piece of stone. The rapid flow of lines fascinated the boys and in a few minutes they could tell how their seals were going to look.

While Ish was making his sketches, Nari had drawn Yarem to one side and was talking to him earnestly. She felt, she said, that their attire was incomplete because they had no necklaces. The boys had realized that they had none but their costumes were new and they had been too busy getting used to wearing them to think about necklaces as part of their proper dress. Now when Yarem suggested that the boys ought to have them, Ar said, "But Yarem, I already have one. You were there when the Pharaoh sent it to me. Surely you remember!"

"How can I forget," said Yarem smiling, "but that necklace is much too fine for everyday wear, Ar. And what about Pta?"

Jewelry from Crete — ear ring, necklaces, seal and gold flower

Nari had been listening, and without more ado, she said to Ish, "They will have necklaces — now!"

Ish bowed. Nothing would be simpler, he said. From a chest he brought out trays of necklaces already made up. Nari pointed to one at once and said they would take it. And they would take that one. There! Neither boy questioned Nari's choice. Wearing their necklaces, they left the shop, well pleased.

Many more people were moving about now, for the business of the day was well under way. As they passed one shop after another, the boys were inclined to fall behind, there was so much that was new to them. But when they saw a foundry, they were completely fascinated. Nari insisted, however, that the foundry would be there another day, and the day after that. They had planned to go swimming and swimming they would go!

They had barely arrived at a small sandy beach not far from the city when Nari, like a flash, was in the water. They had seen Yarem dive and swim the afternoon before, and thought him expert, but compared to Nari, his movements seemed positively awkward. Nari circled Yarem like a sportive fish, disappearing underwater here, coming up for air where she was least expected, and then doing it all over again. Dolphins appeared and played about them. Her laughter

Spearhead and dagger. Man pouring bronze casting for a double axe

rang out across the water at this token of good luck.

Ar and Pta finally set timid toes into the waves that curled on the beach, wishing with every step that they were somewhere else. There was a vast expanse of deep blue water in front of them, while the golden shore of fine sand behind them was a solid, comfortable place. Suddenly Pta sneezed. "The glare of the Sun God warns me to go back, Ar. I will never go against the warning." Armed with that fine excuse, he splashed back onto the beach. Ar wished he had thought of it first, but it was too late now.

Nari and Yarem cut back through the water to call that his swimming lesson was about to begin. They placed their hands beneath him, telling him how easy it was — "Simply move your hands and feet, and there you are — swimming!" said Nari. Ar tried obediently, and there he was — underwater! He came up sputtering and choking. He had swallowed quite a lot of sea water and felt sick. "All right," Yarem told him after six or seven duckings, "that is enough for the first day." They waded ashore and rejoined Pta to sit in the sun while Ar got his breath back. Nari wandered toward a smooth, flat stretch of beach, took a short run, leaped, and turned a lovely free somersault in mid-air. Yarem watched her idly but made no comment to indicate that he thought the performance unusual. The boys, however, were astounded. Nari repeated the performance. Apparently this was a daily exercise with her — she was not showing off — it was routine. When she dropped to the ground beside the boys, she said, "Well, I think I'll be in good enough form for next week."

"What for?" asked Ar.

Nari looked at him incredulously. Yarem hastened to explain, "Nari is to perform in the Festival of the Bull. It is one of the most important religious ceremonials in Crete," he said, "honoring the strength and power of the God-King — or Minos, as we call all our kings after the great king who ruled Crete one hundred years ago — Minos — The Maker of Laws."

"Oh! But what will she do?"

"She, and a chosen group of boys and girls, will dance with the bulls. The finest and strongest of all our wild bulls will be in the arena, and — no, I'll tell you no more. Wait and see the Festival. I will not deprive you of the excitement of seeing it for the first time by telling you too much now."

And he wouldn't say another word about it. The boys tried tripping him with clever questions, but Yarem only laughed at them. Ar did get an answer to one question but he got it from Nari. "Is the dance with the bulls a punishment?" he asked and she replied at once, "It certainly is not! It is an honor." Then she jumped to her feet. "Now that I have caught my breath," she said, "let's get to this wrestling. I want to find out how you do it in Egypt."

It was going to be pretty silly, wrestling with a girl, Ar thought. Nor did Pta's amused grin help matters at all. He looked at Yarem but received no help from him. Yarem looked noncommittal. So Ar stood up, faced Nari, and with

Man tying captured wild bull

little feints, tried to find an opening for a hold.
The next thing he knew he was lying on his back.
What had happened? He had no idea. At first he
thought he must have slipped. But there was his
good friend Pta rolling on the ground, trying to

keep from laughing aloud. His efforts not to laugh at Ar were almost more offensive than it would have been if he had laughed outright. Ar sat up slowly. Now he knew. Nari had thrown him! Well, it would not happen again. She was only a girl, after all. Nevertheless, he approached her with greater care this time. When two almost perfect holds had somehow failed, he forgot that Nari was a girl — she was a wrestler! He rose from the ground a third time and said, "All right, let Pta try."

Pta stepped up to Nari with assurance. He was sure that he could beat her, a mere girl, and besides, he had been watching the proceedings. He thought he knew how Nari worked. Confidence, however, was not enough. He took three falls in his turn and then he too gave up. Nari was not boastful. She took wrestling, it seemed, as a matter of course and was neither surprised nor proud of her victories over the boys.

Yarem, who had known full well how this would come out, said, "You must not feel badly, either of you. Nari has been trained all her life for this sort of thing. She has been coached by the greatest wrestlers on the island. You see, she must first go through this period of training and performing, then, when she grows up, she will be fit to take her place among the priestesses of the Mother Goddess."

"Well," Pta commented sagely, "what could we expect from one so protected by a goddess? How could we win against her?" Ar agreed with relief, and Yarem thought to himself that Pta would get along in the world. Nari, however, seemed to have forgotten the whole thing. She was gazing out to sea, watching a pair of ships that were moving along parallel to the shore line. She pointed them out to Yarem who immediately recognized one as belonging to his family. It should not now be sailing in this vicinity, he remarked, because it had set sail only the day before for a long voyage to the East. What was it doing here, heading westward? He decided to return to the city at once to look into the matter so they all started back.

As they approached town, they met a procession leaving the city. "This is not a holy day," Nari remarked with considerable surprise. "Why are the priestesses going to the shrine? What can be happening? Come, we must join them. It is sacrilege to pass them by." She set off at a sharp pace, Yarem keeping abreast of her, the boys following as best they could.

Musicians playing flutes and harps led the procession in a blaze of colored costumes, carrying glowing fruit and flowers. At first it appeared to be entirely a women's group, but as they drew closer, the boys saw that there were men also. They hesitated to go on. "Hurry!" said Yarem impatiently. "Come on!"

Procession of singing men and priestess

"Is it right," Ar asked him, "for us to follow the procession to the shrine? After all, your Mother Goddess is not ours."

"Nonsense!" said Yarem. "She is the Mother Goddess of all the gods. She is the earth, the air, man, beast, good, evil, life and death. She is all! Now will you come?"

Since this seemed to settle the matter beyond any question, Ar agreed to go and soon they had caught up with the end of the procession. Now that they were in the midst of it all, the boys could look around them; the first thing they wanted to know was why all the priests were dressed in the same garments as the priestesses. Yarem told them that this was nearly always the case, and that the custom was traditional for such ceremonies. Everyone moved along in time with the music while white gulls floated in the blue sky. The procession kept growing longer as more worshipers joined. In no time the boys found that there were many more people behind them and they began to feel that they were really part of the throng — that they belonged.

They were surprised to find that their destination, a shrine on the side of the mountain, was nothing more than a shallow gray cave. They had expected wonders, a great building such as Egypt would have had. However, a beautiful robe of

55

purple wool was thrown over the simple stone seat at the opening, and standing in front of it was a handsome, imperious woman. Yarem whispered to Ar that she was the high priestess, Nari's mother. "This means," he said, "that something of importance is happening. Otherwise Lasa would not appear."

The priestess Lasa wore the traditional many-flounced skirt and her hair was dressed high and elaborately on her small, delicate head. White doves were circling about her head and shoulders. The musicians had taken positions now on each side of the priestess, and as their rhythm slowed there was a feeling of suspense. Presently, bearers came with the sacrifice, heaping melons, myrtle, iris, roses in profusion upon the altar, covering it entirely. There was no blood offering. A priest and priestess came forward bringing a great bronze bowl containing incense that billowed fragrant smoke into the hushed throng. They placed the bowl at the high priestess's feet, and she sat down, bending toward the smoke while the music merely whispered. Fragrant smoke enveloped her head and shoulders, and the silence of the worshipers became intense as they waited. Only the sound of the doves' wings brushing the air could be heard.

Finally Lasa rose to her feet and stepped forward to assume an attitude of blessing; she raised her right hand with the palm turned toward the people and held the left so that it was seen edgewise in front of her. Suddenly, as if they had sprung from the air, snakes appeared wrapped about each of her arms which she extended stiffly in front of her. The priestess began to sway back and forth rhythmically and to hum in a low, deep, rich tone. The humming became louder, and without quite knowing when the change had occurred, the boys realized that they were hearing actual words. Nari stood next to Ar. When he moved slightly to relieve the tension of his body, her hand shot out and clutched his arm with a grip that had the strength of a man. After that Ar was careful not to move a muscle.

Now the words became intelligible and Ar listened closely to Lasa's chant: "All that has been, will not be . . . when the sea blazes flames . . . only bronze will quench them . . . water will not . . . Be wise, my children . . . what is spoken, is to be."

The priestess sat down and gazed out across the sea. A long, shuddering sigh passed through the assembly. Then the people turned quietly and went down the mountain toward the city in silence. Nari and the boys lingered at the shrine. At last Lasa straightened up and turned her gaze upon them. "So my daughter and her friends remain," she said. There was a pause and then she murmured, as much to herself as to them, "Twice before this has happened to me. But on those occasions I was unable to hear and understand the message. I was too late with the warnings. But today!" She groaned. "Oh, these are bad tidings. Woe to Crete!"

At last, she rose and came toward them, having shaken off her ominous prophetic mood to some extent. She now appeared as Nari's gracious and beautiful mother. The boys were then presented to her. After what had just occurred, however, no one was in the mood for light conversation. Nari also said goodbye as Lasa dismissed the young people with her blessing. They made their way down to the city where Nari left them for home as the boys turned toward the Artish home. Just as they reached the doorway, Ar accidentally tripped on the rough stone pavement and stumbled against Yarem, almost knocking him down. At the same moment a bronze knife, barely missing Yarem, clattered against the wall and fell to the ground. They tumbled through the doorway and waited inside, wondering what was to come next. Nothing happened. Yarem stepped outside cautiously, stooped and snatched up the dagger. Back inside, he examined it closely. It was of inferior workmanship; it was not a Cretan dagger. It looked like one that could have been made on the mainland, to the north. They started up the half-lighted stairs, Ar still shaken by his brush with the unknown, Pta perplexed and mulling the matter in his mind, and Yarem furious that such a thing had happened in his own doorway. Which of the three was being threatened and by whom? At the landing where they turned, Yarem stopped and said to the others, "Not a word of this to my mother, please. We have no idea as yet what it can mean, and until we do, I would rather not alarm her. But one thing is clear; we have an enemy in the neighborhood."

They arrived on the terrace to find Mother Artish sitting erect on a carved stool. Facing her was — Hatich! "So!" said Yarem, "Nari was correct when she told me she had seen you in the market place yesterday. I take it that nothing less than magic could have brought you here from Egypt so fast!"

Mother Artish spoke, rather coldly: "As temporary head of the family, I gave your cousin his orders. Now I have been asking him why he disobeyed them and returned to Crete. He says that it is because he has had word of your father, who has been away for some months, as I told you. But what I have not told you is that many long weeks have passed since I have heard from him and I have been greatly worried. I thought it a pity to spoil your homecoming by telling you before it was necessary. Now Hatich informs me that your father has gone on a long journey through far lands to the East. Even so, I fail to understand why Hatich found it necessary to come here from Egypt leaving the business unattended when a message could have been sent quite satisfactorily." Her manner was decidedly scornful.

Hatich maintained a haughty silence. He was an extremely handsome young man, although to Ar's taste his eyes were set too close together. He wore a knee-length yellow skirt, a gold necklace and armbands set with rubies, altogether in the height of Cretan fashion. Outlined in the sunshine, he was a fine figure. When he was ready to speak, his answer came in a slow and studied voice: "Mother Artish, I felt sure that you would forgive me when I brought you the good news. The message came just after Yarem had sailed, and I managed by extremely good luck to sail the same day. I was homesick for Crete, my home and my friends. I was also sick and tired of the dirt and ugly barbarism of the Egyptians . . ."

"Hatich!" warned Yarem, glancing toward his guests. The young Egyptians had drawn back at this unwarranted insult and were standing rigid and indignant. Hatich swept an insulting glance over them and continued as though they had never been there at all. "Yarem," he said, his voice raised a little, "I should think you would have little fondness for Egypt. It has seemed most unusual to me that you would bring reminders of your — ah — misfortune home with you, especially strange that you would bring Egyptians into your own home. Or is it, perhaps, calculated as a nice bit of future revenge?" He winked at his cousin. Yarem glared back at him. At this point, Ar and Pta knew just what to do. They bowed to Mother Artish, Yarem and Hatich ceremoniously, turned and left the terrace, leaving behind them an atmosphere that became increasingly tense and strained.

When they had removed themselves, Ar said, "I never considered our being here in that light, did you?" He added, "Of course, I don't believe anything that man says, but it does make me uncomfortable."

"Yes, me too," said Pta, "but you know what they've said about him — that he was sent away in disgrace, almost exiled. In my opinion he is simply a mean, spoiled troublemaker. He's not worth the time we spend thinking about him, now is he?"

Ar's reply was simply to lift his shoulders in the age-old gesture of "who knows?"

A surprise awaited them in their room; they immediately noticed two beautiful chests made of cypress wood inlaid with pale yellow olivewood and black ebony standing against the wall. The boxes holding their personal property had been placed in the center of the room. Now that Ar was to have his own seal, he was doubly interested in noting once again how Yarem had sealed their boxes, and he began to make a careful examination of them. He noticed that the fine carving of the seal was faithfully and clearly reproduced in the wax. That was as it should be, but . . . He moved hurriedly from one box to another. Pta could not understand Ar's behavior until it occurred to him that there might be something wrong.

"Now, what is it, Ar?" he asked. Ar turned to examine the seals on the first chest again. He said nothing. Pta continued, "I hope you aren't brooding because Nari threw you this morning," he said teasingly. If he could not learn what he wanted to know directly, he could usually find out by tormenting Ar about some other matter. Although he drew a response, it was not what he expected. Ar was serious when he said, "Pta, how well do you remember what Yarem did when he sealed our boxes and bales? Think hard, now, and tell me every little detail you can recall, no matter how unimportant it seems. Then I'll tell you what is on my mind."

Pta sighed. "This seems to be a day of mysteries all round, what with daggers being thrown, prophecies, Hatich's arrival and insults," he said, "but I'll try." He walked over to one of their boxes and put his hand on it, closed his eyes, and began, "This was the first one. Yarem took hot wax and put a seal on two sides of it, then one on the front. And this one —" he continued, moving from piece to piece, telling just what he remembered seeing Yarem do when they were sealed. When he finished he noticed that Ar looked even more disturbed than he had at the beginning.

"Whatever is the matter?" asked Pta.

Ar just shook his head.

"You promised to tell me, remember!" said Pta.

"I know I did," said Ar, "but I don't want to say anything right now. Let's wait until Yarem comes in. Then I am going to ask him to do just what you have done. Perhaps that will help me."

Pta knew there was no use coaxing Ar when he was in this mood, so he gave up and said, "Well, anyhow, let's get our stuff unpacked and put away. We can do that much."

"No, that is just what we must not do," Ar said.

63

"We will leave everything as it is, to make sure that nothing can be changed. Let's go to one of the terraces where the family may not be now and see if we can waylay Yarem without anyone else noticing." Pta was still mystified but he went along and presently they were established with a checkerboard, either engrossed in the game, or acting most successfully. There Yarem and his mother found them finally. At once their hosts began to apologize for Hatich's rudeness. Ar looked up from the board politely and said, "Oh, yes, Hatich . . . We have forgotten the whole incident." He succeeded in changing the subject, and when Mother Artish had left them, Ar asked whether Yarem would like to play a game with him. Yarem said he would and moved a step toward the board, waiting for Pta to get up.

"Oh," said Ar, "not checkers. It's a game in our room. We'll show you."

On the way, he explained that they wanted Yarem to play a memory game with them, just for fun, of course. Yarem looked sharply at Ar then and asked, "Why should I play such a game? I remember exactly what I did when I sealed your things." But at Ar's insistence, he agreed to check over everything and when he had finished, said, "Well, what do you want me to say? I think I know, but I'd like to hear you put it into words."

"All right," Ar replied. "As I recall it, this box had three seals, one on each side and one in front. That is the way Pta remembers it also. But now, as you can see, there are two of your seals on the front." He looked at Pta who nodded in agreement.

Yarem's face was grave. "You have noticed something that we were not supposed to have seen. Something is wrong, certainly, and I have no idea what it is. Why don't we unpack together, noting everything that is amiss as we go along? I have my own system of sealing and have had since I was a child. I have always changed the placement of the seals each time. Though the seals themselves are supposed to protect everything, it is a sad fact that even seals have been known to be counterfeited. Let's begin: you will know how things were packed, and I will know how they were sealed."

Box after box was unpacked and everything checked by all three, but nothing was missing or seemed to have been disturbed. Yarem's uneasiness increased as they went along. If the seals had been tampered with, it would have been simpler to explain had something been missing. This way, it was too mysterious for comfort. Mother Artish came in during their search and, noticing the boys' grim expressions, stayed to

65

watch. She knew that something was wrong but
she said nothing. Ar and Pta were scattering their
belongings all about the room and frowning as
they worked. Yarem had come to the last box and
now broke the misplaced false seals. He motioned to Ar, who looked inside and said, "Nothing disturbed." As he removed something with
great care, Mother Artish saw that it was swathed
in the finest woven cotton — a treasure of some
sort, obviously. When he unwrapped it, Mother
Artish could not help exclaiming at the beauty
of the small chest.

"Watch carefully, Mother," Yarem laughed,
"this is only the beginning." Ar opened it to reveal folds of cloth of gold that gleamed in the
light. Mother Artish exclaimed again. Then Ar
folded back the glittering material and revealed
the inner wrappings of fine net, embroidered with
flat ribbons of silver. Inside the embroidery —
was the great necklace! Yarem's mother drew
nearer, speechless at the intricacy of gold and
emeralds that made up the necklace. The huge
emerald scarabs glowed like the magic fire that
sometimes glowed on the masts of ships. The
heavy gold plaques, carved with prayers,
weighted the jewels so that the necklace began
to slip from Ar's fingers. He handed it to Mother
Artish. While she examined it with delight, Ar

66

ran his finger around the inside of the box and stopped in surprise. He drew a roll of papyrus from beneath the silver and gold wrappings. It was covered with writing but the letters were not Egyptian — Phoenician, Cretan, what? He was positive it had not been there when the necklace was packed for the journey. He handed the roll to Yarem, "This isn't mine. I have no idea what it says. Perhaps you can read it — ?"

One of the forms of writing used in Crete

Yarem's eyes ran over the paper hastily. He handed it to his mother, who waited only to give the necklace back to Ar before reading it. "A-yee, a-yee!" Yarem said. "Now we have the answer to all these strange doings, have we not?" He quickly explained the extra seals to his mother who saw at once what the writing implied. "Yes," she agreed, "we have the answer but I do not like it."

"These boxes," Yarem explained to the boys, "were not opened for purposes of theft. They were opened by a traitor. This roll is a gift of death. It discloses the planned sailings of our ships for some weeks to come. Even their destinations are noted and the probable time of arrival. We have a great enemy in our midst. I fear to guess who it is." He looked at his mother. She opened the roll again to check it. "My son," she said, "this list is entirely correct. I am sure that it exactly matches my personal records. Whoever was meant to find it would have a complete working plan of our business. It would be invaluable for . . . pirates." She looked at her son again. Then she said to Ar, "I would like to keep this, if I may."

"It is not mine," said Ar. "I never saw it before. And, I certainly do not want it." He replaced the necklace in its wrappings inside the box. "Should anything come up about this list," said Mother Artish, "it would be better for me to have it than you." She saw no reason at present for stressing how deadly the list was.

"This ties up with something that I saw today," said Yarem. "In the excitement I had forgotten.

One of our ships sailed yesterday for the Far Eastern Shore, did it not, Mother?"

"Yes. It is bound for Phoenicia."

"Was there any reason for its return to port?"

"No, my son, and it has not returned. Why?"

"We saw it and another ship beating westward along the shore today when we were at the beach," said Yarem. "I said then that I could not understand why. Now I fear that I understand all too well. That is another ship lost to the pirates."

"Why did you not tell me this before?" asked his mother.

"Because so much happened today," said Yarem, ". . . and, Great Mother Goddess! I have forgotten to tell you of the sacrifices at the shrine on the mountainside and about Lasa." Quickly he outlined the events of the procession to the shrine and repeated Lasa's mysterious prophecy. If he had hoped his mother could interpret it, he was now disappointed. Instead, she sat in deep thought. It was obvious to all of them that she was troubled. For some time she had been worried about unexplained happenings and now her fears were confirmed. If only she could put her finger on the danger! Seeing that she had forgotten their presence, Yarem said to Pta, "It seems to me that you have been very quiet ever since we came into the house. What is the matter? Don't say 'Nothing,' for I won't believe you."

Pta held his silence a moment longer then blurted out, "It's your cousin Hatich! Remember when the sailor tried to pull me into the shop just after we arrived? I told you then that there was a man inside who was very well dressed and did not seem to belong there. I couldn't see his face, just his golden armband with a red stone in it. But ever since Hatich came here and I saw his clothes and jewelry, I've had a feeling that I'd seen them before. I keep thinking that the man in the cloth shop was Hatich." He looked appealingly at Yarem hoping he had not offended his host.

Ar, for his part, was amazed. Pta had never kept anything from him before in all their lives. Usually Ar knew what was running through his friend's mind as soon as Pta did. "Why didn't you tell me?" he asked Pta.

"I did not think," said Pta stoutly, "that it would be right to talk about Yarem's cousin in Yarem's house. Besides, I was not sure. I'm still not really sure."

Before anyone could say anything more, Nari appeared in the doorway. One glance was enough for all of them to see that Nari was an angry girl. She did not keep them waiting for an explanation, "Yarem, that cousin of yours! I never liked him, but now I can't stand him. I just met him in the market place and the things he said! He started right in talking about Ar and Pta. He walked with me for a while and every word he spoke was ugly and mean. He suggested that they were connected with pirates somehow, else why, he wanted to know, have the pirates been so active recently. And he talked so loudly! Everyone nearby could hear what he said and they knew he meant your Egyptian guests. Some of them began to mutter, and I could see that the fools believed him. That was just what he wanted, of course. In the middle of his remarks, Lysis and Ubi came along — and they too heard what he was saying. Without a word, they came up and stood one on each side of him. They listened and with every word he spat out they moved in closer and closer, finally almost crowding him. There he was, with those two giants beside him; they looked like thunderclouds, too. Finally, people couldn't help it. They began to laugh. He looked so small and they, though silent, were large and threatening, I can tell you. Then he saw the smiles and heard the laughter all around him. He turned almost purple with rage, wriggled out from between the two and left, walking so fast that he might as well have been running."

"Never mind, child," said Mother Artish. "I can do something about Hatich, and I will. He will leave tomorrow and there will be no doubt about his orders. I have had enough of his insolence myself." She went out with a determined gait. Left alone, the young people tried to make plans for the next day, but it was difficult to turn their thoughts ahead. Too much had happened today: pirate ship, Lasa's mysterious words at the shrine — what did they mean? The dagger; who was the intended victim? All in all, no one cared to talk much.

Yarem had so little to say at the evening meal that Pta and Ar began to feel that they might have done wrong in commenting on Hatich so freely. After all, they were guests of the House of Artish. Their hosts seemed increasingly reserved. When the food had been taken away, they all sat silently on the starlit terrace. Mother Artish got up to go inside, moving so quietly that only a whisper of skirts brushing the doorway indicated that she had gone. Then Yarem spoke.

"A ship came in from Tiryns this afternoon," he said slowly. "It brought word from my father. He wrote that he had arrived there a week ago after a long trip overland way from the East. It had been a good trip, and he had done well both selling and buying. About an hour after the message another ship brought a second scroll to my mother. It reported that my father had been found dead, murdered in the house he owns in Tiryns and by someone with a key to that house, for he was found in a locked building. More treachery! Beyond that, nothing is known. This has given me the entire responsibility for the Artish family. Fortunately, my mother and others will advise me."

The boys could think of nothing to say. They had never in their short lives been this close to tragedy. They wished fervently that they had never left Egypt. What could they say to Yarem? How cruel it was that he had not seen his father after his return! Finally Ar said, "We will offer up prayers for the dead."

"Thank you," said Yarem.

In their own country, Ar and Pta well knew, there would have been the customary weeping and wailing at time of death. But here on the island of Crete, at least in the Artish family, it was not so. A deep and heartbreaking silence prevailed in the House of Artish. That was all. The boys excused themselves and went to bed.

Next morning, as soon as they were out of bed, the boys went to the upper terrace and stayed there. They had no wish to intrude upon family affairs. It was here that Nari found them. She had come to go to the beach with them, but when she heard the sad news, she left telling them she would come back soon, after she had found her mother and told her what had happened. The boys sat uneasily, wondering what they ought to do. Then Yarem appeared. He was sad and troubled and they could see that he wanted to talk. They told him again how sorry they were.

"I know," said Yarem, "but we now learn that my father's death was not the end of the bad news. It is most disturbing. The ship's captain has told us that the people of the mainland are gathering a great fleet together. There are rumors that the island of Crete is about to be invaded. In addition, our own navy has been unable to control the sea lanes as it used to, and piracy is increasing. This we three know from firsthand experience. Also, we have had word from another of my uncles that it would be advisable for us to gather together our most valuable possessions and hide them at once in a good, safe place. He says that if this is a rumor only — and he hopes it is that — no harm will have been done. If it is not a rumor — well, we will be prepared. He is not a man who is easily panicked."

Ar looked at Pta, amazed and frightened. Invasion! In this day and age? Invasions occurred only in history and stories! They were still ask-

In the palace of Knossos a procession of worshipers moves from one floor to another while behind them the dolphins painted on the wall swim by. Below, the priestess holding the lily of Crete blesses her friends.

ing questions when Nari reappeared. Following her and moving with graceful dignity came Mother Artish and Lasa.

"Yarem, have you told the boys?"

He said he had. Then he and his mother began to make their plans. For a time the priestess sat and listened. Then she said, "I too have much to do. First, I must go to Knossos and warn the Minos. I will carry to him two warnings, the one from the mainland and the message of the Great Mother. Now I understand the meaning of the prophecy that she put in my words yesterday . . . Whether the Minos will listen or not, I cannot tell. But I fear greatly that he will not heed me. His life has become too easy. He feels so sure that the fortress of the sea is all that is needed for protection now, as it was in the past, that nothing will move him. I will leave just as soon as possible. However, I do not think it wise to excite our people too much even though they too have heard the warning. I shall announce that Nari is to dance the Dance of the Bulls at the royal palace; that will account for our departure."

"Better still," suggested Yarem, "why do you not send properly accredited messengers to the Minos? As you say, the chances are that he will pay no attention. But you will have warned him. Then, as soon as you are ready, follow with Nari as though you were leaving for the festival. By that time, we of Artish may be ready to go with you, Ar and Pta can be moved out of danger, and the whole departure will appear routine — also no undue panic will result if this rumor is not true."

"That is a good idea," said Lasa. "Of course you understand," she said, "that if we are invaded, I must stay here. I belong to the Mother Goddess and may not leave."

Yarem thought to himself that they would see about that. "You can go to the Minos and return, you know," he said, "but I am sure you will want Nari to be removed from danger."

"Oh yes," said Lasa, "that has been worrying me, but with the Great Mother's help, the problem is now resolving itself."

"Then why not announce that you will journey with Nari for the Dance of the Bulls at the royal palace," said Yarem. "Then we will proceed with our plans."

Lasa agreed to everyone's relief, and when Nari started to protest her mother's determination not to flee the island, Yarem looked at the girl meaningfully. His glance clearly conveyed his promise to discuss the matter later. Nari said no more. Presently, however, she began to think about her own plans. She must hasten to get the new clothes for the festival at the palace rather than in Palai-kastro. This she told Ar and Pta, adding, "You will need some too! And new jewelry."

Ar asked, "What's wrong with the clothes we have?"

"Everything," Nari said. "They are all right for every day, but for a gala occasion at the royal court, you must have the very finest. Certainly you would not care to have people pitying the 'poor Egyptians,' would you?"

"You mean we're really going to the court at Knossos?" asked Ar.

"Certainly we are and now let's get busy," replied Nari.

"This is just like home," muttered Ar. "Even when you're threatened with danger — new clothes, new jewelry, new cosmetics, new per-fumes — that's all women talk about!"

Then Mother Artish interrupted quietly, "Nari, it so happens that Ar has brought a necklace with him. It is, I think, the most beautiful one in the world. You need not trouble to find a finer one. Even the Minos will envy him. Ar, why do you not get it and show it to Nari?"

While Ar was gone to fetch the necklace, Pta told its history. His listeners were so absorbed in the story that they did not even notice that Ar had returned carrying his precious box. He

77

sat down and waited until Pta had finished. Then he said, "There is just one thing wrong. Pta seems not to have told you all that *he* did."

"I guessed as much," said Lasa; "there were too many gaps in an otherwise engrossing story." She smiled at Pta. "One thing is certain," she said. "You are a splendid storyteller. We were spellbound. Now, Ar, let us see this wondrous necklace." Lasa's relaxed attitude in addition to Pta's story had done much to relieve the tension of the group.

Ar opened the box and began to unwrap his treasure, being, if possible, more deliberate than ever. He liked the moments of suspense as he unfolded the cloth of gold and the silver-embroidered net almost as much as he loved to see the necklace winking at him with all its green eyes. His performance was duly appreciated and by the time the necklace was revealed both Lasa and Nari were speechless. Ar lifted it and offered it to Nari, but the girl backed away in awe.

"I would not dare touch it," she said.

Ar had never before seen her unprepared to meet a situation. Perhaps he could not wrestle with her, but he could do something else!

"Turn around," he said. "Let me put it on you." Nari looked doubtfully at her mother who nodded. Then she turned and Ar fastened it

around her neck. At once Nari twisted her head,
trying to look down and see the necklace. Yarem
took pity on her and sent a servant to bring a
mirror of polished silver. When it was handed
to her, Nari spent a long time looking at her re-
flection. Lasa and Mother Artish exchanged quiet

Woman with mirror of polished metal

smiles. Then Nari sighed and told Ar to help her
take off the necklace. He handed it next to Lasa
who admired the carving of the scarabs and the
intricate work on the gold plaques. Returning it
to Ar, she told him that she had never seen anything so handsome.

"A treasure like that must not be lost to Ar,"

Lasa said to Mother Artish. "The House of Artish will have to assume responsibility for it if we have trouble. Had you thought of that?" Yarem's mother nodded. Lasa went on, "I have been thinking as I sat here that a time of great evil is surely upon us, and that we must prepare for it. No doubt the Minos will do nothing when he receives my warning. I am afraid that everyone will have to protect himself as best he can. You are fortunate. You have ships in port, and you can get away. It would be best to have them put in at a port on the southern shore. I gather, from the rumors you heard, that the attack will come from the mainland to the north. It seems that our teaching on the mainland has borne bad fruits — for us. Yarem, it is your duty to hide or carry away all that you can of the Artish wealth. I will help you if you will allow me to place Nari in your care when the time comes for you to go and for me to stay. Do not use the secret hiding places of your family. They will be of no use. For years I have known where they are and so must others. We are living in a time of treachery, not of trust."

This surprised and dismayed Mother Artish and Yarem, but Lasa said in parting, "Come to me in the morning, Yarem. I will tell you of a safe place."

Mother Artish would have no time for her grief.

She was going to be busy. Three or four of the Artish ships had made port during the night and were being unloaded in the morning when Yarem and the boys went down to the warehouses. Yarem went to an inner room at once and sent word to have the captains brought to him there. When they came he said, "You are old and trusted friends of my family. It grieves me to have to tell you that my father has gone to the Land of the Shades. Also we have learned that trouble may come to us any day from the mainland. We are going to prepare for possible invasion. Continue to unload your ships, but do not reload. Make some excuse, however, to remain in port. Say that the omens for sailing are bad, that you are in need of repairs — what you will. But stand ready for orders." Then he called for wine, spilled the libation to the Mother Goddess, and drank with the captains to the soul of his father. The captains expressed their sorrow and offered their continued loyalty in as few words as they could. They had been devoted to Yarem's father and were shocked to learn that he had been murdered. Nevertheless, they went about their business as they had when he lived.

Yarem now told Ar and Pta, "We must work fast. We can save only the most valuable articles. The first thing to do is to sell the merchandise we brought from Egypt. The gold we will keep. News has already passed through the port that your cargo is of great value and many here wish to trade with you. You two must go out and buy in the town. There will be no trouble about your credit since the desirability of your merchandise is known. When you think you have exhausted the value of your own cargo, do not stop. I will keep adding to it from my stores. I want you to buy and buy and buy! But buy gems and jewelry mostly. I realize that such steady buying will push up the prices you must pay, but that cannot be helped. We must turn our goods into valuable small items that can be carried away easily. Fortunately, the people of Crete have a great feeling for miniature beauty."

"Would it not be a good idea for Nari to come with us?" Ar asked. "I am thinking of the advice of old Bu back home. You will remember how he said, 'If you go south and want no one to know it, start for the north.' In the same way, if we try to buy one thing and Nari makes us buy another, it will appear that we are not very clever and that a bossy girl can rule us. Such behavior will keep the facts of our forced purchases from becoming known too soon, if at all."

"I think you are right," said Yarem; "try it. I

feel almost as though Bu were leaning over my shoulder . . ."

". . . and why not also have Lysis and Ubi accompany us?" Pta suggested. "I am not afraid myself, you understand, but with all the gems and Nari with us . . . and evil people about . . ." His voice trailed off. He hoped no one would think him a coward, but he had no liking for the crowded market place since he knew that Hatich was still in town.

Nari, Lysis and Ubi were sent for and in a short time the expedition set out. They went first to a lapidarist's shop where the boys began to select cut and uncut stones with Nari's help. As the buying went on, Ish appeared puzzled. He had never known anyone to buy so lavishly, not even the Artish family. Presently he asked a pointed question. "And the credit for these purchases," he said. "Is it to be in goods here in port, or credit in Egypt?"

Ar had to think quickly. He wondered what Yarem would wish him to say. This gentle old man was Yarem's friend — they had seen that the day before — but would it be safe to indicate to him what their intentions were? He decided that Yarem would want Ish to know that there was danger in the air. So he said, "Ish, if you will permit, I think it would be best if you transferred your credit to Egypt."

Ish glanced at him sharply. He had his answer. He looked wise and nodded briefly. Ar tried to maintain his own appearance of wide-eyed innocence and soon completed the transaction. The jewels were quickly wrapped in small cloth packages and given into the care of Lysis. As they left, Ish was rapidly gathering much of his fine stock and packing it into small chests. It was evident he would soon be gone from Crete.

In the same manner they visited three or four more shops, Nari dancing her way between them. She had never had such freedom of choice. But soon word of their lavish buying was known in the market place and it was time for the boys and Nari to remember their theatricals. So they began to disagree about their purchases. Nari chose the finest jewels she could find, the boys disagreed with her and poked fun at her choices, the shopkeepers tried to agree with all of them and close the sales, and in the ensuing pandemonium sometimes the high prices came down! Then the boys would let Nari win, and the game would go on.

Leaving one of the shops, Ar chuckled and congratulated Nari on her bargaining ability. "That was quite a scene you put on," he said.

"His prices were ridiculous," said Nari.

"Were they?" asked Ar. "From what he said he was on the verge of starvation. In fact, all the shopkeepers seem to be starving, their parents are dying, and none of them has less than fifteen underfed children." They were all having a thoroughly good time. Even Ubi and Lysis smiled now and then. They tried to play their own roles with dignity but they had never seen anything as funny as these three young people bargaining for gems.

Nari drew them inside a building colored a delicate pink with a black and gray spider hanging from her web painted on the wall. This, she explained, was a weaver's sign, and this man was the finest weaver on Crete except for the queen's own weavers. She wanted some of his wonderful cloth. They passed through the shadows of the storage magazine on the first floor and went up the stairs to the weaving room where the looms were busy. There they chose piece after piece of fine wool or linen. Then the shopkeeper's cousin came in with some exquisite embroideries and Nari had to have some of those as well. So it went on. Ubi and Lysis staggered away under their loads and Ar realized that their bodyguards could carry no more. Of course, it would not have been fitting for the young buyers to carry anything. They started back home.

Later in the day Mother Artish, who had been checking over their purchases, told them that they had done very well. There were only a few pieces of jewelry that she would not accept. They were of poor quality and would have to be returned. Then she cautioned the boys not to appear excited or tense during their appearances in the market place. "No one must think that we are worried," she said.

Yarem, meanwhile, had gone to see Lasa, and on his return spoke at once to his mother. Lasa had made a map of a new place for him on papyrus and now everyone must study it and then destroy it. On the map was shown a shrine on the south shore of the island, a shrine so close to the sea that one could almost dive from its entrance into the water. There all objects of greatest value were to be taken and hidden under the shrine, where they would be safe. Accordingly, Yarem had started to load the ships. Next day he was going to the market himself and would buy gold and silver cups, platters and armor. He had let it be known that he had an order from the eastern end of the Deep Green for such a shipment. He was outlining his plans in considerable detail when Nari, who had been listening quietly, gasped and fell to the floor moaning. They picked her up and carried her toward Mother Artish's quarters. Yarem shouted for the servants and there was a bustle of confusion and concern. But, as they left the terrace, they met Hatich. He almost seemed to sneer when they said that Nari was sick although his words expressed regret. The Egyptian boys brushed by him, for they had nothing to say to Hatich — yet. They left Nari with Mother Artish and went to their room.

"Whatever happened to Nari, do you suppose?" asked Pta.

"I suppose it was a bad case of Hatich," said Ar. I was looking her way just as she collapsed and her gaze seemed fixed on the doorway. I think she had seen Hatich hanging about listening, the sneak!"

"I wonder how much he heard."

"The gods alone know. We'll find out when it's too late, no doubt."

Yarem came in and heard what they were saying. "So, that's it," he said. "He has just informed me, my fine cousin has, that his departure must be delayed a week. He can prove that the delay is unavoidable, but I wonder . . . Well, I will tell Mother at once and we will change all the plans. Too many extraordinary things have happened when he is about for our comfort." He had no time to say anything more, for a great hammering broke out at the entrance of the house. It reverberated through all the rooms and now a man's voice shouting through the din demanded admission in the name of the Minos. Yarem rushed downstairs, the boys after him. In the main room they found Mother Artish confronting a group of soldiery. The officer in charge was telling her, "My lady, our orders are to take the Egyptians into custody and to search all their possessions. Information has been laid against them and they are declared to be enemies of the Minos."

Ar and Pta were truly horrified and suddenly frightened. They were strangers on Crete. Who could protect them against the mighty Minos?

Nari, miraculously recovered, appeared for a moment in the doorway, saw the soldiers and slipped away again. As Mother Artish tried to protect and defend her guests, four of the soldiers came and stood guard over the boys. They were prisoners! Others went to their room and returned with all their personal belongings. Chests and boxes were dumped on the floor, opened and emptied. When they came to the beautiful box that held the necklace, Ar shuddered. He could not, he must not lose the Pharaoh's gift! He started forward but a guard jerked him back. The coffer was opened, the cloth of gold and the silver net were pulled out roughly, and finally the box was overturned and shaken. Ar hoped they would

Warriors of Crete

not break it. But there was no sign of the necklace! Mother Artish sighed softly in relief, and Ar
felt that his knees were buckling. What could
have happened to the treasure? At least, the

soldiers had not got it — but who had?

Mother Artish's fury had been mounting. Now, blazing with anger, she confronted the officer in charge. "How dare you do such a thing in my house, to a guest of the House of Artish? I hope for your sake that you are merely following orders, for the person who instigated this insult is going to be sorry — very sorry! As you can see, there is nothing here to threaten the safety of the great Minos, or anyone else! Just two boys from a distant land who are our guests! For shame, to war on boys!" Ar and Pta did not like being called just boys but they were still too frightened to take exception. Boys, indeed! Actually, inside they both felt like little boys and nothing could have pleased them more than if their fathers could have walked into the hall at that moment. Then Ar thought, I am an Egyptian! He straightened his shoulders and stood tall. Pta did the same. Mother Artish was still having her say. "I am sending for the High Priestess Lasa at once," she told the officer, "and we will see what she has to say to you!"

This was too much. The officer shifted his weight from one foot to the other uneasily, cleared his throat, and said, "My lady, I cannot help this, I assure you. I but follow orders. These boys, we have been told, are in the pay of the pirates. Furthermore, they have concealed in their possession a necklace that none but royalty could own. Of course they have stolen it — or perhaps the pirates stole it and gave it to the boys to keep. At any rate, they have it and we must find it. And our orders are to take them into custody."

Now Yarem, who had been silent because his mother had had so much to say, spoke in a cold forbidding voice. "I protest this move. Speaking as the head of the family of Artish, I will not permit my guests to be taken from this house. I will, however, guarantee that they will not leave it themselves. You may post guards here, but that is all you may do. I have spoken."

"But, my lord," said the officer of the guard, "this I cannot understand. It is one of your own family, your own cousin, who has laid the charges against them!"

Yarem and his mother were stunned. Then Yarem exploded: "How can such a one speak for my family, when he is no longer a member of it? He is a private individual and we no longer own any connection with him, none whatever! Now, go away! The charges are rubbish!"

"But, my orders . . ."

"Your orders are — to leave this house at once!" said a stern, rich voice from the doorway. Lasa, the High Priestess, stood there terrible in her fury.

"I have spoken," she said, "now go!" Her outstretched arm indicated the way. It seemed to the young officer that sacrificial smoke encircled her — certainly she was forbidding. He had been uncomfortable with Mother Artish and Lord Yarem; now the intercession of the priestess was all that he needed to reduce him to a very nervous young man indeed. He was glad to go away. He bowed, paused only to command two of his soldiers to remain as guards over the Egyptians, and left quickly.

Lasa said to the family, "Just as Nari came to me, I was questioning a sailor. I have been wondering how to tell you that Hatich is the traitor. But now you know and I need not be the one to inform you. He had expected to become head of the House of Artish himself, and finding himself thwarted in this, I imagine he has decided to reap his profits from the Artish family in another, less honorable fashion. Next, I suppose that Ar is concerned about his necklace. I have it in safekeeping. Nari brought it to me when she found there was to be a search. Tell me at once what plans Hatich could have overheard."

Ar and Pta exchanged glances. So that was it; Nari had seen Hatich and pretended to faint. Shortly afterwards she had seen and heard the soldiers. She had had time to remove the necklace. Yarem explained what plans had been made to Lasa, who listened intently. Then, when he had finished, she said, "I suggest this: load the ships with everything you would not mind losing too much were the island invaded. You will leave the house in good order, but everything that can be safely carried will be hidden on the south coast."

Meanwhile the two boys and Nari had been whispering to one side. Ar interrupted. "Tell them your plan, Nari," he said.

"I had thought," said Nari, "that we might make double use of the trip to Knossos. Since it is to be a royal occasion everyone would expect us to take a great train of luggage. We could also take many servants without arousing suspicion. All this would be expected of us and attract no particular attention."

Her ideas were acceptable and further plans resulted. Mother Artish said, "It will give the young people additional reason to go to the market again for the next two or three days. When one visits royalty, much is needed; everyone knows that. All they need do is advertise our destination. The ships," she added, "can be loaded solidly but with nothing of great value. Perhaps, this way, the caravan may escape with our fortunes."

"Fine!" said Yarem. "We will start out with an enormous caravan. I will even hire extra horses and many extra litters. Also I will use only the most trusted sailors as servants. Then, at a given point along the way, I will find it necessary to delay some of the company. Those left behind will, of course, be responsible for hiding the goods we wish to store at the shrine while the others will continue toward the palace." The plan seemed workable and everyone agreed to it.

Next day, however, still another ship arrived from the mainland laden with treasure that Yarem's father had amassed on his eastern buying journey. This valuable cargo presented another problem: there were bales of cloth soft as swansdown and cobwebby as the work of spiders all in glowing red, blue and green. There were objects of strange and intricate pottery work and most curious, small bottles. The bottles had delicately painted pictures inside them and stoppers made of carved jewels. A scroll of papyrus from Yarem's father explained that these were most precious and had come from a great distance; the people who had made them, he had written, were small, yellow and slant-eyed. Yarem pondered silently over this information of far lands received after his father's death. It was doubly precious to him now, and he meant to preserve this last shipment with his life if necessary.

Thereafter, everyone was frantically busy but still they kept up the pretense that this activity was merely routine preparation for a visit to the Minos. A search for Hatich had been undertaken as soon as they had definite proof of his guilt, but so far it had been fruitless. Hatich had a gift for disappearing and reappearing. The unloading, sorting and reloading continued unabated.

The second day all was ready, ships were loaded, the caravan was assembled, the plans were all understood and the map destroyed. But the ships did not sail — this was according to the plan. Mother Artish left orders to delay their departure until nightfall on one pretext or another — perhaps she was undecided about something, or it might be that she wanted changes made. At any rate, by this device, sailing would not take place until it was dark and the unusual hour of departure would seem to be due to her vagueness. The ships were to set out for the northeast as though they were headed for the mainland. Then, later at night, they were to change their course and turn south, sail around the end of the island and anchor off the southern shore near the shrine of the Mother Goddess.

Those setting out with the caravan would start in light chariots, followed by the long train of pack horses. They would pretend to be merry and lighthearted as befitted guests setting out to a royal festival, for Mother Artish had not announced the death of her husband.

Still nothing had been learned of Hatich. This was the only unfinished business — the only matter that could not be planned.

The ships set sail, accordingly, that evening. The chariots and pack train started at sunrise the next morning. Many friends of the Artish family were on hand to say goodbye and to wish them luck. To close friends Mother Artish had hinted of danger — it had seemed right to warn them, — but such was the pleasure-loving mood of the Cretans that they paid little attention to her warnings. They decided that she must be emotionally disturbed. Why else would she be carrying a basket with kittens in it!

The friends went their carefree ways. They had been safe for a long time, and if the Minos showed no worry, neither would they. Mother Artish wished that they might have believed her, but admitted to herself that her flight could never have been so easy had the whole town realized the danger. Well, she had tried! It was just like the fable of the man who knows there will be a flood and moors a boat in his garden. The neighbors deride him for a fool until the waters rise. Then they despise him because he has a boat! Mother Artish decided to concentrate on the success of their own plan.

Before they left the Artish house, Ar and Pta had searched for the guards who were supposed to watch them, but the soldiers were nowhere in sight. Lasa smiled quietly, and the boys had seen enough of her power to accept the situation without further question.

Progress through the town was slow because of the busy morning activities. All was as usual except that when they passed the gem shop of Ish, they saw it was closed — even the sign was gone. When they gained the open road, no one hurried to make way for them. There was plenty of time in Crete that morning.

From the main stone-paved roads stretching from one end of the island to the other, smaller roads branched toward the right and left. On the outskirts of the many scattered villages were patches of garden with watermelons and cucumbers ripening in the sun. The thorny evergreen gorse was in a glory of yellow blooms, and the silvery foliage of the olive trees marched over hills and small mountains. The wind from Africa helped everything to grow with its gentle warmth.

Throughout the land were springs with groves of tamarisk, pine, and laurel trees. Each grove and spring harbored one of the many shrines of the Mother Goddess. They made a practice of stopping at each shrine to give an offering. In this manner the slower-moving caravan was able to keep up with the swifter chariots. The boys had been surprised that there were so many small villages and towns so close together. Taking advantage of all the stops, Ubi and Lysis had kept the caravan and travelers together.

Toward evening Lasa decided that it would be better not to stay at any of the towns or villages. They would camp beside one of the shrines away from the main roads and so avoid notice and speculation on the part of the townspeople. Further, it would prevent any loose talk among the servants living in the towns. The camp chosen was in a grove of dark green cypress trees. Around the spring and the edge of the small brook that it formed, myrtle was growing and flags were still in bloom. The crocus had come and gone, but in the early spring the hills and mountains were covered with this flower. A small fire was built and the kittens were let out of their basket to play and frisk about. All the servants, fascinated with the small lively animals, stood watching and laughing at their antics.

Crocus and other flowers of Crete

After everyone had eaten, another council was held. The next morning the travelers and the treasure caravan would have to separate. Nari suggested that perhaps it would seem plausible if the boys announced that they were not feeling too well; Lasa, naturally, would order them to remain in camp. Nari continued: "I will remain to help take care of the poor suffering visitors."

Lasa had begun to wonder just how trustworthy the Artish sailor servants were, and Mother Artish said, "They are all trusted men who have been with us for many years. We have never used slaves for just that reason. Slaves, in the nature of things, think of their freedom first and loyalty to their masters after that." She glanced lovingly at Yarem as she spoke. It was still incredible to her that this imperious son, now the head of the House of Artish, had been a slave in Egypt. She went on, "If you wish to be sure of them, Lasa, you are at liberty to bind them with an oath of silence. You are the High Priestess."

Just to be sure, Lasa thought she would. She called everyone together and after a blessing and a prayer, accompanied by proper sacrifices of fruit and flowers, she began an intonation in the flickering firelight: "Be it known, one and all who are here in the presence of the spirit of the Great Mother, never will a word be spoken of what is to happen within the next few days. The power of the Goddess is ever present and to speak will not be death, for that is too easy, but rather, should you speak, you will be struck down with pain and sorrow that will follow you through a long and miserable life. Come, place your hands upon the altar and swear that your silence will be eternal, in so doing you will receive the blessing the Great Mother gives." This was quickly and solemnly accomplished. Then everyone slept for a few hours.

When they awoke, according to plan, Ar and Pta complained that they did not feel well — perhaps the fast ride in the hot sun, perhaps something they had eaten . . . "Please," they begged,

Priestesses with sacrifices

"could we stop rushing so much? Can't we fall behind a little until we feel better?" After a little discussion, making sure that everyone was able to hear what was said, Mother Artish, Lasa and Yarem went on ahead, leaving the boys and Nari,

101

Ubi and Lysis to follow more slowly. Thus if any questions were asked on the road they would all have the same story. Later, when the others were well out of sight, those remaining reloaded their horses and proceeded in a leisurely manner toward the shrine on the southern shore while the others traveled westward.

Ubi thought they would reach their destination about the middle of the afternoon, which would give them time to unload before dark. "We will take everything to the shrine," he told the boys. "Lasa has revealed to me the way to get at the caves under it. To anyone who might observe us it will appear that we are simply bringing everything into the shrine. Then, when all has been carried in, I will send the sailors back to their ships. When they have gone, we ourselves will hide the treasure in the secret caves below the shrine."

Matters turned out as Ubi had planned, and when the sailors were headed back toward Palaipastro in the late afternoon and safely out of the way, Ubi and Lysis approached the stone altar. "There is so much to do," chattered Nari, watching as the two powerful men grasped opposite corners of the altar and strained toward the right, "I don't see where they can store all of these things."

"Shh," said Ar. "Watch."

Bringing every muscle to bear, Ubi and Lysis strained at their task. For a minute nothing happened. Then, with the grinding sound of stone upon stone, the altar began to move and slowly shift its position. When it had made a quarter turn, the men stopped to draw breath. Ubi called to them, "All three of you had better help us. Get on Lysis' side and push against the top with him. You must tilt the stone toward me. I will stay here and keep it from sliding over too fast." So Nari and the boys pushed and shoved and gasped, and Lysis continued his own considerable efforts quietly until at last the altar began to tilt. Ubi used a small log to lower the altar and in time it thudded to the ground revealing a stone cleverly fashioned to work like a pivot lock. Looking down where the altar had stood, they could see a flight of shallow steps leading into darkness. Ubi collected enough twigs and dry material to start a small purifying fire at the mouth of the cave. When it was apparent that the air was pure, he told Lysis to open one of the larger bundles which held pine torches. Making sure that each of them held a lighted torch, Lysis trod out the fire carefully and Ubi led them down the stairs. The way was uncertain in the flickering light with the darkness always ahead, but they found that along the wall holes had been gouged from the rock itself and Ubi directed the others to stand their torches inside them. They went down about ten steps and emerged into a large chamber suitable for storage purposes. Other torches had been left in holes in the wall here, and having lit them they went back up the steps to bring down the bundles and boxes and bales. Down and up again they went, Ubi and Lysis carrying the heavier loads, the boys and Nari hurrying with the smaller things. It was long after dark when they finally carried the last loads to the hidden room. Since they intended to spend the night at the spring nearby and Ubi and Lysis would take turns on guard, there was no need to struggle to set the altar back in place until morning.

They made a simple camp and took time only to care for the horses before lying down. The boys and Nari fell asleep almost at once; they had worked hard for several hours and were weary. The grapes Nari had been eating fell from her hand; the camp was quiet. Lysis, who had taken the first watch, prepared the chariots for an early morning departure but was careful to make no noise; by the time he came to waken Ubi, nothing had disturbed the silence. Ubi's watch was uneventful and at dawn he wakened the boys. When he approached the blankets where Nari had slept, he found that she was gone. But before he could realize how frightened he was to find her missing, he saw Nari coming toward him, her arms filled with iris. "These flowers are for the Great Mother," she said. "I thought I ought to gather what I could find to put on the altar before we go away." The sun had come up behind her, outlining the girl and her load of purple and gold flowers, and bathing land and sea in a luminous mist.

They were ready now to set the altar back in place, but Ubi had noticed the horses moving restlessly and he was disturbed. He looked about but could see nothing that might have caused their uneasiness, so finally he joined the others in the shrine. Even though replacing the altar was much easier than removing it, the sun was well above the horizon before they had finished. They must be on their way. Nari placed the flowers upon the altar and murmured prayers. Ubi and Lysis harnessed the horses.

As they finished, without warning something swished overhead and they found themselves suddenly enmeshed in a network of ropes such as were used to catch the wild bulls that roamed the island. They could not fight ropes, and the more they struggled, the more tightly they became entangled. It was maddening, particularly as they

Hunting net in use

could hear men shouting and Ar screaming, "Run,
Nari! Run!" Ubi and Lysis were trussed up in
the nets and, strong as they were, they could not
fight back. Ar and Pta were tied up too, but Nari
was nowhere in sight. The four of them lay roped

This design shows the Mother Goddess of
Crete. A young warrior makes his offering.
Notice the symbols of Crete, the bull and
the double axe.

upon the ground unable to move until their assail-
ants came and stood them on their feet. Then
they saw that they were in the hands of a band of
blond sailors who pushed and shoved them ahead
and laughed at their fury. It was the easy success
of their capture that disconcerted Ubi and Lysis,
powerful men who could never have been taken
in a fair fight. Their captors talked in a strange
language that Ar and Pta had never heard. Lysis
had, however. It was his own native tongue, the
language of the mainland to the north. Since
these men were sailors, Lysis and Ubi were not
surprised to be bumped and kicked down the
rocky hillside to the shore. The boys got somewhat gentler treatment, but it was still rough. No
one knew what had become of Nari. Offshore a
ship was anchored — a pirate ship. The sailors
dumped their captives into a small boat and
rowed them to the ship. They were pulled aboard
without ceremony.

The first person Ar saw was Hatich, standing
next to the captain of the pirates. "They have
caught Hatich too," he said to Pta.

Hatich overheard him. "They have not, Egyptian puppy!" he said. "It is I who have caught
you! And where is the brat of the priestess?" He
had waited in particular anticipation to see Nari
brought aboard, a miserable captive. "Where is

she?" he repeated. No one answered. In fury he strode to the leader of the sailors and drew back his fist as though to strike. But the captain quickly interceded, grasping Hatich's arm and twisting it. Caught off balance, Hatich almost fell; his knees bent and Lysis laughed for the first time since the ropes had fallen around him. "The traitor must bend the knee," he said in his own language. The captain laughed involuntarily at this, and Hatich seethed with fury. He had come aboard as leader and now he was finding that the captain intended to command the ship! He must gain control at all costs, he knew. He pulled himself together.

First, the captives must be humiliated. He turned to Ubi and Lysis. "You two good-for-nothings will do for the oars," he said contemptuously. "We'll make use of your brute strength all right. But first there are things I would learn from you. As it is, I know much already. There are only a few details . . . One of the ships from Palaikastro was captured. So I know that my fool of a cousin was trying to move treasure, even though there were only goods of little value on board. Now you are to tell me what has become of the real treasure. Where is it? We searched the cave of the shrine. Nothing there!"

Ubi opened his eyes wide and assumed as

stupid an appearance as he could. "Treasure?" he said in an affected high soft voice. "What would a servant know of treasure?"

"You two would know," said Hatich, "because for years you have worked like dogs for the Artish witch, that is why! She's had something to do with this if I know her. And you have done her bidding like the stupid fools you are. Now tell me what has been done with the treasure."

"We are but servants," answered Lysis. Hatich could get no more from him and hesitated to try violence because he was not sure what the captain would do if he struck either of them. Perhaps these boys —

"Well, you little Egyptian pigs, if I know you and your debased race, you would not lose sight of your own treasure! You must know where your own property is! You have been buying enough goods in the market to pay a king's ransom. Speak up and tell me what has been done with it, you scavengers!"

Ar and Pta stood as straight as they could despite their bonds and replied not at all. They did not intend to reveal the hiding place, and their case seemed so hopeless that they did not see how it could become much worse. They kept silent.

Hatich sneered. "There are ways to make you talk, never fear." Then he directed that Ubi and

Lysis be taken below, given oars and set to work. "We will go for a small pleasure trip," he said, "not far; we'll come back here this evening. By then you'll be willing to talk."

The gong began to sound and the ship gradually got under way. Hatich ordered ropes to be tied around the boys' bodies, just under the arms. The net that had enmeshed them was kicked out of the way, but they were still under guard. Before they could enjoy the freedom of moving their arms and legs, Hatich said something to their guard that they could not understand and they were hustled to the stern of the ship and lowered over it toward the water.

Hatich came and looked down at them as they dangled. "So! Little desert rats don't like the water? Yes, there are ways to make them talk." He laughed, and at a signal they were dropped nearer and nearer to the water. They were thoroughly frightened, but while that leering face looked down at them, they tried hard not to struggle. They could not help twisting and turning, however, as they felt the water rising over their bodies. When it had reached their chests, Hatich gave another order and walked away. Thus they were trailed behind the moving ship, fearing every moment that they would be dropped beneath the surface of the sea. Presently, the ropes began to swell and tighten around them until they could hardly breathe. This discomfort soon became greater than their fear of the water. Just as they thought they could bear it no longer, they were hauled back on deck, dripping and miserable. Hatich came and questioned them again. Still they refused to speak. "Then it's back into the sea with you," he said, "and you'll be tied with fresh ropes, too. Don't think that I forget anything."

He walked away; the sailors tied them up again and dropped them back into the sea. The gong beat, the ship continued to move ahead and Ar thought how desperately Ubi and Lysis would mind it if they knew that their efforts were helping to pull them, half drowned, through the water. The boys were barely conscious when they were pulled back the second time. Hatich let them lie in their dripping and torn garments on the deck for a while. There was little use torturing boys who did not know what was happening to them. Nor could they be questioned. There was time for two or three more duckings, however, before evening approached and the ship was finally turned back to its anchorage. But Ar and Pta had not answered a word to the repeated questionings. When Hatich at last left them in disgust, Ar did manage to whisper to Pta. "Now

111

I know who threw that dagger. It was Hatich, I'm sure." Pta nodded. He hadn't the strength to do more than that.

Hatich was sure that the treasure must be hidden somewhere in the neighborhood of the capture. It would have to be searched next day, and the prisoners must be made to talk. Right now it was time for him and his pirates to eat. There was nothing, however, for the hungry prisoners who had not eaten all day. They were left on deck by Hatich's orders, which were given in the Cretan language so the boys could understand. "There is no place for them to go, so leave them there," he said. "Dead or out of their minds, they are useless to me. Let them perish of slow starvation if they chose not to loosen their tongues. It is all the same to me, but a little time to think might make them willing to talk." He walked away.

This was all that Ar needed in the way of a hint. Half dead as he felt, his busy mind was beginning to function again; there had to be a way out of this. So Hatich thought they'd lose their minds? Well, perhaps that would be a good idea!

"Listen, Pta," he whispered, "I am going mad!"

Pta turned toward him at once. Worried and frightened enough already, he had counted on Ar to keep his head. "Mad?" he asked. "Why, Ar, you have been in worse fixes than this — well, almost —"

"But I am going to be mad, and you are going to be terribly frightened because I am," said Ar. And with that he at once let out a bloodcurdling shriek and then burst into laughter that was wild and shrill. After that he sang, off key and without rhythm. When Hatich and the captain came in haste, as Ar had felt sure they would, he appealed to them as gods to come protect him and started to sing a hymn of thanks. He kept this up for some time; then, as they watched mystified, he switched to a humming of lullabies. Pta took his cue almost at once and, when a favorable moment offered itself, pleaded that Ubi be brought to them: Ubi could do something for Ar, he insisted. The captain gave the order at once and soon not only Ubi but Lysis appeared on deck. Ubi and Lysis had to come together, for their ankles were tied so that one could not move without the other. But the presence of both was more than Ar had cared to expect. He went on with his performance. Whether or not Ubi knew what was going on, he hastened to Ar, picked him up and soothed him as though he were a baby. Ar continued to giggle and weep by turns but quieted gradually as though Ubi's attentions were helping him.

Hatich, meantime, watched the scene closely, finally satisfied that the performance was real. He could not believe that all of them could trick him unless there had been a chance for rehearsal. At last he said, "Leave them together. We have no room for them anywhere else on the ship and there is no way for them to get away. But keep them guarded. Useless Egyptian rats," he said scornfully over his shoulder as he turned and went off. He had succeeded in nearly breaking the spirit of these proud youths, and in this he found satisfaction. He didn't care much what happened to them for the rest of the night. Tomorrow was another day. He would learn the hiding place of the treasure, come what may. Perhaps he had pushed Ar too far . . . ? Well, he'd worry about that tomorrow.

With the departure of Hatich and the captain, the guards relaxed and moved far enough away so as not to be disturbed by Ar's antics. Ubi went on crooning to the boy, whispering now and then a few words and phrases. He had not been fooled; he knew that Ar was entirely conscious. Now to get themselves out of this fix. Ar, in turn, alternated bits of information with his fretful ravings. He was too clever to drop his role all at once. Yet Ubi learned all that had happened and that Ar was determined to escape. All four were

114

in agreement on this; they must get off the ship. But how?

Time passed, the darkness deepened, the guards dozed, and the four captives tried their ropes, eased themselves where they could, and rested as well as they were able. By pulling hard on the boys' ropes, Ubi managed to loosen them enough so that blood could circulate normally. In the midst of these efforts, Ar felt Ubi stiffen. He looked up quickly and chills ran down his back when he saw, white against the dark water, a human hand!

It seemed to be attached to nothing, and rising high above the waves in the background, it held a long dagger! Promptly Ubi clamped his hand over Ar's mouth and stifled the gasp that was forthcoming. Then tugging Lysis along, Ubi inched over toward the railing. By this time, Pta, who had followed the sudden movement, saw the hand also. As he started up, Ar silenced him as he had been silenced. The boys watched breathlessly as slowly and quietly the two men, tied together, worked their way over the deck inch by inch. When they reached the railing, Ubi reached out in a flash and seized the dagger, which was held level with the deck. At once the hand disappeared. Ubi cut the thong that bound him to Lysis and then motioned toward the sleep-

115

ing guards. Passing the dagger to Lysis, he indicated in pantomime what must be done. Lysis nodded and moved toward the sleeping men without a sound. Ubi blocked off the boys' view with his great body, but they heard a soft thud and then another and guessed what had happened.

Lysis knelt to wipe the dagger on the guards' clothing. There were two soft splashes before he came back with more precious weapons. He cut ropes that bound the captives, and in complete silence he and Ubi led the boys to the side of the boat and motioned down toward the water that flowed beneath them.

Ar shuddered — go down into that? And not even dangling at the end of a rope? He wished for his bonds back again. After all, he could not swim. He had thought it bad enough to hang at a rope's end in the sea, but now to be told to jump into the waters was just too much! He had had all the water he wanted. He couldn't do it; that was all. But while he was thinking all this, he saw Lysis slip overboard; nothing but a slight splash indicated that he had gone into the water — that and a slowly widening ripple. Then Ubi picked up Ar and dropped him over the side holding him by a wrist. He whispered, "Take a deep breath and hold it." Ar had no choice, so he breathed deeply and Ubi let him fall. The water was cold and he seemed to sink down and down in the blackness forever. A hand clutched his arm. He gulped water in his panic; surely now the sea witch Scylla had him! But somehow he was on the surface, choking. As he gulped the welcome air, however, he was still trying to keep as quiet as possible. "I am holding you," a familiar voice said. It was Nari! "Lie on your back and I will pull you along. It's too bad you Egyptians shave your heads, but I'll cup your chin in my hand. The others are coming."

These were the last words Ar heard for what seemed hours — hours of trying not to panic as he was drawn through the water, knowing that if he gave way to fright he would become as heavy and inert as a stone, hoping that Nari could manage to get him to shore. Finally he heard the unmistakable sound of water lapping against the beach. The impulse to make for this safety was almost his undoing — he jerked and sank beneath the water. Again, Nari's hand cupped his chin and Ar's panic left him. After a few more strokes she released him and Ar felt himself sinking. Almost at once he touched bottom. He was in only two or three feet of water! He struggled to his feet and could not think when he had known a more welcome sensation. Discreet splashing near him indicated that the others were coming in also.

When they reached shore, they sprawled there exhausted for a moment and, looking out across the water, they could see men with lighted torches dashing back and forth on the deck of the ship. They had been missed already!

"Hurry!" said Nari. "They will be after us in no time." She led them away from the shore up a hill. When they reached the top, they began to recognize their surroundings — they were back near the shrine. The chariots were still there, and the horses were still harnessed to the chariots — ready to go. Nari had thought of everything! Ar found it hard to believe that a girl could think out plans for so daring a rescue and then bring them off. But now she was outlining further plans. "Ubi and Lysis must take the chariots," she said, "and each must start off in a different direction. Yet each must make sure to turn and head for Knossos to get help for us. We will wait here." At once Ubi and Lysis protested. The girl had rescued them, they knew, and she had done it well. But now they felt perfectly capable of planning their escape and they felt sure that Yarem would expect them to protect the boys and Nari. It was no part of their routine to take orders from a young girl who was not even one of the family to whom they owed allegiance.

Nari, however, was not the daughter of a High

Priestess for nothing. At their first murmurs she drew herself up and said, "I have told you the plans. They will be carried out! You see I have had all day to think of what to do and to worry about all of you. In that time I have turned over in my mind every possibility. So now I know what is best. This is the only place where we can stay and not be found. We three will remain right here. You will help us move the altar as before and tilt it just enough for the three of us to squeeze through into the cave beneath it. Then you, Ubi and Lysis, will let it fall back into place and move it around until it locks in position. Food and water are already in the shrine; I have seen to that. All we have to do is to carry it below."

There was no time for further discussion, since the voices of the pirates could be heard across the water and from all indications they were coming ashore at once. Ubi and Lysis had no more objections; indeed it would have been hard to plan better than Nari had. They all ran to the shrine and took hold of the altar. The stone turned, tilted, and Nari and the boys slid into the cave beneath it, the food and water were passed down to them and the altar was tilted back into place above them.

They sat down on the steps in the dark and

realized all at once that Nari had not quite remembered everything — she had forgotten to plan for any light. They were in thick, heavy darkness. Overhead, no doubt, the chariots were thudding away carrying Ubi and Lysis; at this very moment, most certainly, the pirates were stepping ashore and beginning their search. On the steps, in the inky darkness of the cave, the three thought of these things, shuddered, and drew closer together. As a matter of fact, their clothing was still wet, and it was cold in the cave. They talked in whispers, as though the pirates could hear them through the solid stone.

"I do hope Ubi and Lysis got away in time," murmured Nari.

"Do you think the pirates can find out how to turn the stone?" Pta asked.

But Ar said, "Why would they think of it? They do not know it turns."

"That Hatich is so evil he seems to find out everything," said Nari shivering. With one idea the three made their way to the bottom of the stairs, keeping touch as they descended.

Once down they felt more secure, but it certainly would have helped to be able to see! When they remembered their food and water, they felt their way back up the stairs, groping carefully in the dark. They got back to the bottom all right, and began to feel that the darkness was a little more familiar than when they had first come below the altar. They talked together more calmly, sitting on the bottom step with a water jug between Ar's feet and bundles of wheaten cakes and fruit in Nari's lap.

"Now," said Nari, "tell me what happened from the time the pirates threw the nets over you."

Ar told her quickly, for she already knew the beginning and the end of the tale, adding, "Tell us what you did! How did you get away?"

"It was easy," said Nari. "Your warning saved me. I had a chance. You were taken by surprise, but when you yelled to me to run, I ran! I ran as though all the evil demons and witches in the whole world were after me, and what chance did a pirate have then? I got so far ahead of them that they gave up. Then I hid in the olive grove — that old sacred grove where the trees are so gnarled and the branches so twisted that no one can get through them quickly. Finally, when it was safe, I stole out and saw the pirates on their way down the hill to the shore. But when I saw the four of you all tied up and pushed into the boat, I thought I should die. It seemed bad enough, to know that all of you had been captured and that I was alone, but when the big ship was rowed from the anchorage, my heart really sank.

Then I noticed that the ship was only circling and that it seemed to keep in sight of the shrine all the time. I watched and saw you dropped into the sea and then decided that the pirates intended to come back to the anchorage. That meant, I knew, that they would also come ashore sooner or later. I tried to think what they would do when they landed and then I began to make my own plans. I wanted you back on shore, but I did not want the pirates to come with you. So I thought and I plotted — and you know the rest."

Ar shuddered. "I'll never forget how I felt when I saw that hand with the dagger come out of the water. There was nothing else — no body, no head. Ugh, it was fri — it was a surprise," he said.

Nari chuckled softly. "Well, my plan worked."

"Yes," said Ar, "and you saved us."

"Now what shall we do?" Pta wondered.

"We can't just sit here," said Nari, "and we won't even know when it's daylight again if we stay on this spot. Let's do something."

"I know what I want to do first," said Ar. "I'm starving."

"So am I," said Pta.

"I haven't stopped to eat either," Nari admitted, "except for a little fruit."

When they had eaten and drunk, they felt better. But the heavy darkness had become oppressive, they were restless. With one accord, they scrambled to their feet and began to feel their way along the wall. "This reminds me of the time when we were shut up in that tomb, Pta," said Ar.

"Yes, but that time we found a way out. I hope we can get out of here," said Pta, "and let's not lose one another."

"Don't leave me!" said Nari. "Let's stay together." This was the first time she had shown any panic. Ar reflected that she had never been shut up in the dark before. He and Pta had. "We've got to explore, Nari," he said. "If we don't know what is around us, waiting for the others will be even harder."

"Explore! How can you? You might as well try to fly!" exclaimed Nari, inconsistent in her momentary fright.

"There's a way of exploring in the dark," Ar told her. "We've done it. And we're better off here, really, than when Pta and I were in the mastaba. We've been here before. I noticed when we were storing the goods here that there were some passages or tunnels that led out of this chamber. We can feel our way along the wall until we come to one, and we can all hold hands."

"All right," said Nari, "I'll go if we all keep

together. If one of us were alone and fell into a hole, the others might not even know it."

The boys agreed and they continued their blind search along the wall. It seemed to go on end-lessly and they began to wonder whether it would ever end or turn a corner or do anything! Finally Ar, who was in the lead, called, "I've found some-thing — an opening!"

But Nari had another objection. "So we go in there and get lost," she said. "No one will ever find us. The others will come back and search, but we'll never be found. I don't like it." She hung back.

Pta, who was on her other side, agreed with Nari. "I'd hate to stay in this dark hole forever and ever," he said.

"And I thought you were the brave smart boy!" said Ar.

"Well," said Pta, "if you are smarter, just tell me what we are going to do."

"Why," Ar said, "I'm going to explore, that's all. I'm not just going to stay in one spot until I drop."

"I know what to do," Nari said suddenly. "Take off your belts."

"What on earth for?" asked Ar.

"They are padded and rolled, aren't they?" asked Nari. "Well, they are stuffed with twisted cord. We will take our belts apart, pull out the cord and wind it into balls. Then we will fasten the end securely to something at this end of the passage and unroll Ar's ball as we go along. When his is used up, we'll tie the end of it to mine and follow that. When mine is gone, we'll use Pta's — and by that time we'd better be somewhere, for there'll be no more cord. If we decided to turn back, all we have to do is to follow the cord."

The boys had their belts off and were pulling out the stuffing before she finished. It was hard to straighten the cord in the darkness. However, squatting on the floor of the cave, they succeeded. Their knees ached when they got up. Walking back into the chamber they felt all around for something to which they could tie their cord. A small heavy chest seemed the best choice, and having accomplished this task, they started off again.

"How did you think of this, Nari?" asked Ar, feeling his way along the wall.

"To be truthful, I got it from a legend they tell on the mainland," she said. "I heard it long ago. It seems that a hero of theirs, Theseus, was sent here to Crete, as a sacrifice to the Minotaur — a monster, half man and half bull, that belonged to the great Minos. Anyhow, Theseus didn't want to be sacrificed and he attempted to escape. But he became so confused trying to find his way out of the great labyrinth of the royal palace that he couldn't get anywhere. Along came a princess named Ariadne, who pitied him or something, and gave him a ball of cord so that he could tell where he had been by retracing his steps and trying again." Nari went on with the story as they groped along the passage, but Ar interrupted her to say, "We're at the end of this passage. Now what?"

"We might as well try again," said Pta. "Go on, Nari."

"Wait," said Nari. "What happens here, Ar?"

"This one just ends in a blank wall of stones it seems," said Ar, "so we wind up our cord on the way back just like Theseus in the story."

"And we go back and find another passage," said Nari. "So when Theseus found he was lost again . . ."

Through the second tunnel, Nari told them how the Priest-King, represented by a bull, died a symbolic death each year at the festival and then was supposed to return to life as the husband of the Mother Goddess. That accounted for the religious rites at the festival, she said.

Ar had become much interested in the story and the similarities in some ways of the religious beliefs of Crete to those of Egypt. "It is the same with our god Osiris," he said, "and his life and death." He would have gone on to explain had not Nari interrupted excitedly, "Hush! What is that sound?"

"It sounds like the sea — far away!" said Ar after a little pause.

"And a little breeze is lifting my hair," said Nari.

They all wanted to rush forward, but the business of unwinding the cord was slow. Nevertheless, it had to be done. The passage itself was becoming smaller — lower but no narrower. In a minute they found that they had to get down on their hands and knees and crawl to get through it. They did not mind, however, for the sound of the sea had become unmistakable. Ar passed the cord to Nari who was last in line.

"You'll have to unwind it now," he said. "Creeping over it tangles it so that we'll never be able to back-track unless the last one unrolls the ball."

Here the passage turned and they began to see daylight, faint and far away, but undoubtedly daylight. How many hours had passed since their escape in the night? They kept on, as fast as they could crawl.

"Light and air," gasped Nari softly. They reached the opening at last and found that here there was room enough for them to sit abreast and look out. They were high above a small beach. The cliff, near the top of which they were resting, stretched out on both sides to form projecting arms that enclosed — far below them — the little sea beach, and formed a small cove. For a time, the three simply looked their fill at the sky and water. The sky was blue and bright and the indigo water, sparkling in the morning sunlight, looked nothing like last night's black depths. All three drew deep breaths.

Nari was the first to speak. "Look!" She pointed to the far left and, following her finger, the boys leaned out of the cave and saw the pirate ship! They instantly pulled back but laughed when they realized that it would be almost impossible for them to be seen from the ship. Cautiously they moved to the opening again. A boat was pulling out from the ship, heading toward shore. Were the pirates off to search for them again? The small boat passed out of sight for a while and then reappeared heading back to the ship from the shore. This time the three observers groaned together. For in the boat, again trussed up, were Ubi and Lysis! They had been recaptured. Now, who would tilt the altar stone and get them out of the cave? Worse still, there was no one left who knew where they were. Behind them was the

darkness of the cave. In front of them, the sea
. . . and the pirate ship.

They were tired, thirsty, hungry and discour-
aged. For a long time they sat just inside the
opening, their backs to the sea and sky. Now and
then one of them sighed. Finally Nari sighed a
sigh to end all sighs. "If only Scylla, the sea
witch, would attack that horrible ship!" she said.

"She might kill Ubi and Lysis; that wouldn't
do," said Ar.

"No, I suppose it wouldn't," said Nari.

Suddenly Pta had an idea. "It's very simple,"
he blurted out. "All we have to do is get ourselves
out of this cave."

Ar poked him in the ribs. "Is that all?"

Nari giggled and said, in a high mocking voice,
"We'll just pick up and leave, then. Just how do
we do it, Pta?"

"By using common sense," said Pta calmly.
"We know we cannot get out by way of the altar.
Good! But we have found this opening."

"Fine! So we just tumble out and land in the
pirates' laps." Ar was disgusted.

"Wait a minute," said Nari. "Pta may be right.
There's a good deal of water between us and the
pirates. Besides, they don't know we are up here,
so they aren't looking here to find us. They are

going to hunt around the shrine for us, not up on the side of this cliff or in the sea. We can climb down the face of the cliff and swim around the point."

"By this time," said Ar, "you must have some idea that neither of us knows how to swim. I should think you would . . ."

"You can't wrestle either," said Nari with some of her old sparkle. "All right, so you can't swim. I can. I will get down, swim around the point away from the ship and go for help. I will merely have to find the local priestess and she will send a message to my mother. She will hide me so I will be all right. The only thing is that you two may get a little hungry and thirsty before I can get back if I am not as lucky as I hope I will be."

"First let's see what they are doing on the ship," said Pta. What he really wanted to see was how anyone could get down the face of the cliff. "Nothing seems to be happening on board," he reported. "They are staying, that's all." Then he looked below him. "Nari, you can never make it," he warned. "It's too dangerous."

"Starving is dangerous too," said Nari.

"Besides, they will see you," said Ar.

"I'll wait until dark," said Nari, "but I'd rather go in daylight. I don't want to catch hold of a bunch of spiny cactus."

That, Ar thought, was the least of her problems. They sat in the opening for what seemed hours watching the clouds skitter across the sun which seemed to blaze unmovingly in the same spot. The waves slapped on the beach below. They wished they dared to eat again and help pass the time, but food and water had to be carefully rationed. They hardly realized it when the clouds covered the sun, and mist began to come in from the sea. Looking up, Nari shivered. "I'm chilly. Where is the sun? Oh, look, there's going to be fog! Wonderful! I can go now and not possibly be seen."

It was no use to object. Nari repeated that the fog would conceal her and if she hurried, she could still see enough to find footholds as she went down. She crept from the opening and lowered herself over the cliff. The boys held their breaths, but she found a footing and her head dropped below them. They leaned over watching her descend slowly and surely. Then the fog rolled in so thickly that she was soon lost to them in the damp white mist. Had she got down to the beach? They had heard no sound of rolling stones or of anything falling. She must have made it. The waiting began.

Night came and the boys withdrew a little from the opening and settled just around the turn where they had more room and could keep a little warmer. There was no sense making their way back farther along the passage; here, at least, they would know when night ended and day came. In the great storage chamber they would know nothing. They dozed and wakened throughout the night, and in the morning, when the misty sun appeared, they hardly knew whether they had been awake all night or had slept for hours. Time seemed endless.

They crept again to the opening. The fog was lifting. There was the ship, and there was a boat putting in to shore. That was — it must be Hatich rowing frantically toward shore. As the boat disappeared behind the promontory, Ar gasped, "Pta, look at the ship!" Everyone aboard seemed to be rushing as though the sea witch herself were after him, the bronze gong was beating out a fast, although faint rhythm. Now the oars were all in place and they could see men cutting the anchor ropes.

"It must be serious if they risk losing a valuable anchor," said Pta. "I wonder what is going on."

"I think we're going to find out. Look, look, look! And look!" Ar cried, pointing out to sea.

There were four vessels bearing down on the pirate's ship, two from the east, two from the west, moving in on the pirates. They were the smaller, bronze-beaked fighting ships of the Royal Navy. Until now they had been hidden from the boys' sight by the two arms of the cliff.

Now the four small Cretan vessels closed in on the large ship from Mycenae, which was well under way by this time, but the lighter craft were gaining. The boys hoped that they would not all be out of sight before the battle began. Luck was with them, and from their strategic position high above the watery arena, they now watched the fight. The pirates had decided, apparently, to stand by and let the Navy ships come on. The pirate captain executed a quick turn and succeeded in ramming one of the smaller ships; this maneuver the boys had seen before. Now there were three attackers left. Two of them had managed to grapple the pirate boat, but the boys could see nothing of the boarding action — the ships had drifted behind the cliffs. Ar thought of Ubi and Lysis and began to pray. Whatever happened, they must be saved! He invoked the Egyptian goddess Isis and the Cretan Mother Goddess, to be doubly sure. Then he saw the three ships reappear and felt sure the Royal Navy must have won the battle.

The ships turned in toward land and passed out of sight again behind the promontory: there was nothing more to see. The boys concluded that now it might be best to return to the large chamber. If the Navy had won, they would be rescued and rescue would come by way of the altar at the direction of Ubi and Lysis. They didn't allow themselves to dwell on the alternative but followed the cord and crept back along the passage. At the foot of the steps they found the jug still holding a little water, and two wheaten cakes. There was no more fruit. They sipped and nibbled slowly because if no one did come to rescue them, they would need every drop and every morsel. They sat and talked about the battle, wondering just what had happened. It seemed darker here than ever, their eyes had grown so accustomed to the brightness of sky and water, and unconsciously they spoke in whispers. Waiting seemed harder than before. Time passed as though it were carried on the back of a snail.

Pta said, "We must have been sitting for hours — and I am dying of thirst."

"Well, even if you are, we must save what food and water we have until we are thirstier and hungrier." At that moment, they heard a slight scraping sound above their heads!

They started up the steps as the altar thudded to its side and they could see, silhouetted against the light, Ubi's head! He was smiling a great, wide smile, and Lysis of the golden hair and beard was beside him. The Royal Navy had freed them and they were uninjured.

"Nari, is she with you? Is she safe?" both boys asked simultaneously.

Instantly then Nari appeared also, laughing happily. "Of course I am," she said. "Come out of the cave! Let us close it and go away. We will not need to come back to the treasure for a long, long time. It will be safe."

When they approached their chariots they were met by a group of young priestesses who had brought them food and drink. Ar and Pta reached for it eagerly. Then Ar drew back his hand and said shyly that he felt they ought to offer a thanksgiving sacrifice on the altar before eating. After this was done, they ate and Nari told of her climb, swim and search which had been successful. And now, if they were finished, they ought to start for the King's Palace. There was still time, she said, to cover a good part of the distance in daylight. It seemed odd to Ar and Pta that there was any of the day left; the hours in the cave had been so long. But apparently, it was the same day.

They traveled steadily until dark, rested for the night, and traveled again. In midmorning they came to a circle of stony hills, forming a wide valley with a river flowing through from north to south. There were cypress and cedar trees dotting the hillsides, and here and there small flocks of white sheep browsed on the scattered vegetation. Within the circle of the hills was the wondrous labyrinth that was the palace of the Minos. The bottom of the valley was a carpet of rainbow-

View of the palace of Knossos from the southwest

hued wild flowers and spread far and wide on the carpet was Knossos. They paused to admire the splendid sight, and saw two chariots race out of the palace gates and up the road toward the hill where they waited. Richly dressed young noblemen in both chariots greeted them, then turned spiritedly and led the way back to the palace, while their own vehicles followed right behind.

Lasa, Mother Artish and Yarem waited just within the gates, where the little party was welcomed joyously as soon as they stepped from the chariots. The newcomers were escorted through courts and corridors, in and out of great rooms, past workshop after workshop of artists and craftsmen, until the boys were overwhelmed by all the magnificence. Overwhelmed and even a little frightened; this was beyond anything they had ever dreamed, this sprawl of buildings, all this splendor! Painted walls, and columns that were small at the bottom and large at the top, stairways and more color, more painted walls, unending! They were glad when finally they arrived at rooms in the men's quarters and were provided with the baths they needed so badly. Rubdowns followed with aromatic oils and new, clean clothing of luxurious materials to wear. They had long since lost their wigs; their hair had not grown much in a few days and they felt rather

Man pressing wine and pottery storage jar

embarrassed. Yarem suggested that they fashion
headdresses such as were worn in Egypt. Cloth
was provided and somehow this was done. The
boys felt more presentable. Yarem informed them
that there would be a ceremonial dinner later in
the day in honor of the Priestess Lasa, but he
thought there would be time to talk over their
adventures before the dinner. They were guided
to a terrace where the women waited for them,
but Lasa and Mother Artish had hardly settled

The tapering columns of the small temple are resting on symbols of the bull's horns. Soldiers guard the temple while the animated crowd discusses the agility of the dancers and the power of the bull.

themselves to listen when court dignitaries began to join them. So much ceremony was involved in the introductions that followed that the whole story could not be told after all. Mother Artish looked at the young people apologetically while the elaborate courtesies continued. Then, before they knew it, the time came to go back to their own quarters and dress formally for the state dinner. They all felt a little frustrated. The danger of invasion remained but formality took precedent.

Back in their rooms the boys examined the still finer clothing that now awaited them and marveled at its quality. Yarem, helping them with their strange and wonderful attire, asked a steady stream of questions. "What of Hatich? Were you badly mistreated by him? What happened to him, do you know?" Before the boys could answer, a servant brought in the cases containing their two necklaces: Pta's carnelian necklace and Ar's magnificent emerald and gold one. Between fastening them around their necks, putting golden bands upon their arms, and struggling to get their headdresses properly adjusted, they managed to tell Yarem what they knew.

"Well," said Yarem, "all that I know definitely is that he was not among the prisoners taken."

"I feel sure that we saw him going ashore in a boat just before the Cretan ships attacked the pirate vessel," said Pta.

"No doubt he is hiding somewhere here on the island," Ar surmised. "His kind always seems to manage to get away before the ship goes down."

Further conversation was forestalled by a message from Lasa directing them to come to the Great Hall as fast as they could. The king was about to make his entrance and if they did not come at once, they could not be admitted. So they hurried through the corridors and came to the hall well filled with people. They wore clothes of brilliant hues, golden ornaments and magnificent jewels.

The place seemed like a home for the gods.

"I never saw anything like this in my life," whispered Pta. "How many people do you think there are?"

"Shh," Ar urged.

"Maybe two hundred?" Pta could not be silenced.

Ar nodded and moved his lips as he tried to count the kaleidoscopic throng. But he had to give up; people moved about too much. He nudged Pta as four young men, dressed in crocus yellow, appeared at the door leading from the Royal Quarters and, raising huge conch shells

to their lips, blew a hoarse, musical blast to announce the king's approach. At once the guests
fell silent, faced the doorway and bowed deeply.
The Minos and his queen entered. The king, sur-

Man blowing conch shell as king enters

prisingly, was a withered little old man, so elaborately dressed and bejeweled that Ar and Pta
leaned forward searching to find the man himself
beneath all this panoply. Instead of his bearing

141

the young queen on his arm, she was helping him for he was very feeble. Was this, then, the king whom Lasa was risking her life to warn of danger?

At the far end of the room in front of a painted wall the Priestess Lasa stood waiting. Behind her dolphins swam through a painted sea. Other priestesses stood on each side of her holding lilies which were waved rhythmically to the music of the softly played harps. Lasa straightened to her full height and seemed to grow taller as she moved forward and sang a prayer of benediction. The Minos nodded his appreciation.

Soon great platters of food were brought to the tables and the guests were directed to be seated. There were quantities of beef, mutton, goat, and many varieties of fish, all of them immersed in richly spiced sauces. But a special delicacy were the onions, which Ar was much surprised to see Lasa eat. At home in Egypt, the priests used onions for sacrificial purposes and never ate them. He was hard put to make a choice from all the foods passed to him — bread, honey, cheese, fruit, and endless servings of wine poured from beautiful pottery containers into gold cups. The Cretans, apparently, lived for the present and while there was food and wine, did not think of any danger that might threaten them in the future.

At intervals, when he glanced in Lasa's direction, Ar noticed that she appeared thoughtful and weary. He asked Nari about this when he got a chance, and Nari said, "Alas, the Minos refused to accept her prophecy. He would not even permit her to bring Mother Artish to tell him of the warnings from the mainland." She dropped her voice to a whisper and added, "Mother says he is too old and has become too lax through easy living. He laughs at the idea of danger coming to Crete. He thinks it impossible when he sees the luxury in which his people live. Mother thinks the island is doomed."

"But, Nari, did she not tell him of all that has been happening?"

"Oh, yes, she told him. He found her tale interesting, he said, but nothing to take seriously or to worry about. Mother says he has entirely forgotten that to rule a people means also to protect the people!"

Lasa caught Nari's glance and shook her head warningly. They stopped whispering. Gay conversation continued all around them. The aristocracy of Crete ate, drank and played. There were no troubles in their world. Presently the

Minos and his queen rose and withdrew from the hall bringing the dinner to a close.

Nari parted from the boys as soon as they left the hall, saying that next day was the Dance of the Bulls and she had to be ready for her performance. She had been to see the bulls that day: great, powerful creatures, she had said, especially netted for the occasion. They should provide a splendid spectacle. Realizing that Nari actually intended to go through with this, the boys were more impressed with her than ever. Since they had been in the palace, they had seen wall paintings of such events and were anxious to watch the dance. Any fears they might have had previously about Nari's risking her life in such a manner had been completely dispelled by her recent activities. They knew she could take care of herself. Right now they were too weary to worry much about tomorrow or even to anticipate the festival. All they wanted at the moment were soft beds and warm blankets. Once they had their wish and drew the blankets up to their chins, they thought of the cold stone they had slept on the night before and the hard wet deck. Cushioned in luxury, they fell fast asleep.

A fanfare of conch shells and trumpets woke them next morning. The sun had barely risen, but the palace was in a ferment of activity. The

144

boys bathed and dressed hurriedly to be ready when Yarem should come for them. He came immediately, and they lost no time in getting to the theatrical area where the dance was to be held. The arena was a natural bowl, formed by one of the hillsides which encircled Knossos; seats by the thousand ran in tiers up the slope. These were for the ordinary citizens; royalty and nobility occupied thrones and stone seats near the floor of the bowl. These were covered with soft wool-filled cushions in lovely colors. Yarem looked about him appreciatively but Ar and Pta gaped frankly. Egypt did not have a theater. Yarem told them that many of the religious festivals which the Cretans celebrated, as well as other varieties of public entertainment, took place in this and similar arenas.

"Yarem!" Ar asked, "what, by the god's grace, are those people doing above us? Look, they are hopping, first on one foot, then on two! Women, too!"

"Oh," said Yarem looking around and smiling, "they are playing a game called hop-to-scratch. You see, there is a pattern scratched into the stone of those broad steps and it guides their movements. They toss a stone and then start hopping according to a set pattern. They entertain themselves endlessly with the game until the festival begins." Sure enough, the game was going on along many of the broad steps. Funny people, these Cretans!

"I'd like to play the game," said Pta. Ar wasn't sure; the people looked a little silly to him. He wished the dance would begin.

With another blast of conch shells and trumpets, it did. Instantly the crowd fell silent and watchful.

The festival was opened, of course, with a procession. Nari led the line of young men and girls who came in dancing the beautiful, controlled ritual. Their swaying steps reminded the boys of the long-stemmed lilies that grew throughout the land and swayed with the wind in a stately dance of their own. The rhythmic line moved right past the king and queen without any recognition of their presence at all, to the boys' astonishment, and proceeded to a point in front of the Priestess Lasa where it stopped. There they broke into song, accompanied by lyres, flutes and small drums. While they sang, their dance continued, weaving in and out, their movements indicating that the Mother Goddess was venerated as the mother of the earth, sky, of all growing things, of man and beast, good and evil, life and death. The ritual finished, Lasa blessed them and they wound their way dancing to the other side of the

146

arena. A sigh of appreciation passed through the assembly, and everyone was quiet for a moment before leaning forward to watch for the next event. Now an enormous, heavy-shouldered wild bull was released. He came plunging and charging into the bright sunlight. Bracing his powerful forelegs he stood and stared around. He had been penned long in darkness and all this light, these people, were a shock to him. Wondering, hesitating, he was nevertheless a picture of complete and dangerous power — he could become an unpredictable agent of death and destruction. Was this, Ar thought, hardly daring to draw breath, to be Nari's companion in the ritual dance? She must be insane to think of doing such a thing! He shivered with apprehension, wished he need not look, and yet found his gaze glued to the bull. Nari appeared looking small and frail in her short tunic but she seemed amazingly unconcerned. She'd better take care, thought Ar. He leaned forward.

The bull had discovered the intruder. Nari approached him, dancing in a swaying forward movement. The bull, snorting and pawing the earth, lowered his head to charge. He headed straight at Nari, his wide-spread horns seeming to grow wider and sharper as he came nearer to the slight lilting figure. Except for the thunder

147

of his hoofs, there was no other sound in the arena. The spectators watched breathlessly and waited. Then suddenly Nari leaped forward effortlessly and grasped the bull's horns. His great shoulder muscles tensed and he tossed his head to throw the girl into the air. Nari seemed to rise with the horns and to float in the air, and as the bull passed under her, she made a complete aerial somersault and landed lightly on the ground behind him. The bull whirled round and again Nari danced forward to meet him, grasping his horns as before, and again being tossed. But this time she varied her performance and landed on the animal's back. She rode thus for a few of his lumbering steps, quickly snapped into another somersault, and so to earth. Then, before the audience could fully realize that she was unscathed, she disappeared through the exit as though she were thistledown.

Other boys and girls followed Nari, repeating her exploits. More bulls were released, more dancers came on, and they leaped and turned in the air over the bulls as though it were all mere fun or a game. The bulls charged and pawed the ground, lunged and snorted to no avail. But still, still there was always the possibility that someone might be hurt . . . The Egyptians had never seen such a contest between brute force and skill. The

Cretans were used to it and enjoyed themselves. At the end of the performance, the crowds streamed out of the arena chattering about the bulls and the dancers. Quite obviously, Nari was the favorite. Wrestle indeed! No wonder that girl had thrown them!

No sooner had they reached their own rooms than Lasa appeared. They began to tell her how much they had been impressed by Nari's performance, but she had no time to listen. What she had to tell them, she said, was more important.

"You are to leave the palace at once," she said and her manner was that of the imperious High Priestess rather than Nari's mother. Nari had come in and now stood, pale and frightened, just within the doorway. This was the hour she had dreaded. She knew it by her mother's manner. Lasa went on giving orders, making no acknowledgment of Nari's presence. "Everything is prepared. You will all leave for the south coast this afternoon. Right now you are to go out for an airing in your chariots, that is all. But do not come back!" She gave Ar a bundle. "Your royal necklace; I took it from the box — it will be easier to carry. I will remain here as I forewarned. This is the day of judgment for the kingdom of Minos. The hour approaches. How our fate will arrive, I know not. Today I saw that man of ill omen,

Hatich. Murder and treachery are among us. Something to eat has been prepared for you, but do not linger over it. The horses and chariots are waiting." They were dismissed and they knew it. Then Lasa acknowledged her daughter's presence for the first time. "Nari," she said, "you are also going to Egypt. But first I must have a few minutes alone with you." She raised her hand in blessing and swept out of the room. Nari went with her.

Quickly, those who were left gathered their possessions into small inconspicuous bundles, ate their light lunches and prepared to depart.

Then the priestess came back. "Now leave at once," she said, "and do not stop for anything! Rush like the wind as soon as you lose sight of the palace. Before that, act as if you are merely going out for pleasure. A cloud of dust is rising in the northwest! If you have not left in a few minutes, you will not be able to go at all. On your way to the gates you may be stopped and told that the Minos commands you to an audience later. Acknowledge the honor but pay no attention at all to this order! *Go!*"

Her agitation was apparent and now, when she drew Nari to her for a last farewell, her heartbreak was evident, too. But she said no more, only held Nari in a close embrace. When Nari was released, she drew her fingers lovingly across her mother's robe before she turned to go out with the boys. She said nothing while they hurried through the corridors but as they approached the palace gates she urged, "Hurry! The king's messengers may catch us if we do not." Then she added, "Chatter! Be gay! This is a pleasure ride, remember." Mother Artish and Yarem, approaching from another direction, waved and nodded to friends they recognized in passing; they played their parts well. Ar and Pta, who knew few people, smiled and talked eagerly together, hoping they were acting as though they were setting out for a picnic. But for poor Nari, who had never really thought she would have to go away and leave her mother, it was a hard role indeed. Still, she was equal to any situation; her laughter rang out and she waved gaily to her mother as they drove through the gates. Lasa stood at the top of a long flight of steps, blessing them in the usual manner. So it was that they left the great palace of Knossos, Yarem and Mother Artish in the first two chariots, Nari next, and the two boys bringing up the rear.

They proceeded in a leisurely manner until the rim of hills was crossed and they were out of sight of the palace. Then they raced along the roads as though the invaders from the mainland

Woman in chariot with soldier saluting her departure

were right on their heels. After about three quarters of an hour at this pace, Yarem emerged from what had seemed a stationary cloud of dust ahead and stopped the other chariots. "You are fairly safe now. I must go back," he said. "I have not forgotten Lasa, Nari. Keep going and I will catch up with you." Mother Artish started to remonstrate, but Yarem had gone before she could stop him. "So be it; we will go on," she said and her chariot led off. The others followed and soon resumed their breakneck pace. Two hours had gone by and half of another when Ar, looking behind him for the fiftieth time it seemed, saw Yarem. "Here he comes," he shouted ahead to Nari. "Let's wait."

But Yarem was approaching at a frantic rate of speed. They had never seen a chariot move so fast. As he drew nearer, he waved at them so violently, signaling for them to go on, that they jumped back into their chariots and began to race along as before. As Yarem overtook them and passed each chariot, he shouted, "Keep moving! No stops for anything unless it is to rest the horses! The palace is in flames. I never got there!" The five chariots clattered and thudded along the road; fleeing for their lives now. Yarem had drawn abreast of his mother and occasionally those behind could catch a shouted word or two that was carried back to them on the wind. "Fire and smoke," they heard Yarem say, "everyone streaming out of the burning city," "panic," "revolution or invasion, I couldn't tell which," "murder and looting."

Nari, who had heard all of this, now sped ahead to Yarem. Mother Artish had taken the lead beyond him. She leaned out and called to him, "My mother! Did you see her?"

Yarem shook his head grimly. "No!" he shouted, "the palace was in flames."

Nari moaned to herself. Then truly her mother's daughter, she called again, "She was right! and the Mother Goddess spoke truly!"

Pounding hoofbeats marked their progress. They had all narrowly missed death, and they knew it. They owed their lives to Lasa. Yarem looked over his shoulder once or twice and began to slow his pace. As the others swept past him, he shouted, "Don't slow up! Someone is following us. Keep on!" But his mother's chariot now dropped behind his, and when he called and motioned to her to keep up with the rest, Yarem noticed her mouth was set in a grim line of determination. Looking back, he could see that his mother had wrapped her reins about the upright and that she held in one hand a small coffer which she was opening with the other. Suddenly, she threw a jewel box out on the road, and chains, necklaces, rings and brooches scattered and blinked in the dust behind her. Unwinding the reins, she again took control of her chariot and had soon passed Yarem, calling over her shoulder, "If they are enemies, there is plunder for them!"

Smiling at his mother's ingenuity, Yarem added, "And if they are enemies, they will stop for it; if they are friends, they will come up with us. We'll see."

The fast pace continued with everyone stealing glances behind him when he could to see whether they were being pursued by friends or foes. The road climbed a hill, and the horses began to labor and breathe heavily. The downgrade would be easier for them, Yarem knew, so when they had topped the hill he shouted, "Stop!" And Pta, coming up from behind, said, "They are enemies all right. They have stopped!" Looking back, they could see men clustered along the road, scrambling in the whirling dust for the jewels. From this height they could not see quite as far as Knossos. There in the distance, however, a lowering cloud of smoke hung over the site of the city. It was a man-made cloud. Yarem said suddenly, "Look, look! Two more chariots are coming. Hurry, we must go on!" He jumped into his chariot, curled his long whip above the horses' heads and was off again. The others followed, their horses galloping down the hill, their chariots swaying and jouncing at the pace they held. Even after they could see no one following, they held the pace for two more weary hours, not daring to do otherwise.

At last, when they felt reasonably safe, they stopped to make camp. The horses could go no farther, certainly, and neither could they. They had to rest. The horses were unharnessed and rubbed down carefully, then staked out in an olive grove where they could not be easily seen. The chariots were pulled out of sight behind the grove of trees but kept in readiness for a quick departure should it be necessary. Darkness was falling and they would be hard to locate should anyone be hunting them. The boys volunteered to divide the night watch after bringing water from a nearby spring for the horses.

Ar's was the last watch and long before dawn, according to Yarem's instructions, he awakened everyone and they prepared to go on. There was nothing to eat and no time for food if they had had it. The horses, reharnessed, moved restlessly in their traces, the bronze ornaments clinking just enough to cover the sound of approaching horses. But Pta, whose ears were sharp, had heard something. He moved quickly to his horse's head and motioned the others to do the same. With their own horses quiet they were able to hear the steady beat of hoofs. Yarem and the boys pulled out daggers and loosened their swords instinctively. Ar saw that even Mother Artish and Nari held slender Cretan daggers in their hands. They, too, were ready. The sounds drew closer and their tension mounted. Even if they were not discovered in the olive grove, the thought that they might be permitting enemies to get ahead of them when they knew there were enemies behind was disturbing.

"Not so bad," Ar whispered, "only two chariots. And the horses are about done for, I can tell." The chariots were now very close. Nari peered from the grove. Then she screamed piercingly, "It's my mother! It's my mother!" and flew out into the road. She used the technique she had demonstrated in the arena and stood directly in the path of the chariots. If it proved to be her mother, and she was sure it was, she could dart aside just in time — but she would have halted her. If these were enemies, no doubt she contemplated somersaulting over the horses' heads. At any rate, she stood in the road as the first chariot came up and stopped. Those in the grove heard Lasa's rich voice ask, "Nari, are you alone? Where are the others?"

Everyone rushed out into the road and surrounded the chariots. For a moment there was joyous confusion at the incredible reunion. Then

Lasa said, "The Mother Goddess has saved us all, else we would be dead along with the Minos. There was black treachery inside and outside the palace. The king was murdered in his bath. Palace guards turned traitors; pirate forces from the mainland stormed the palace and got inside with no trouble at all. There was nothing but blood and death in the palace! Fires broke out everywhere and hundreds burned. I could do nothing. No one would listen to me! So the three

Minos, or king, at the ritual bath in the palace of Knossos

of us — Ubi and Lysis are with me — escaped through one of the secret passages. We took your route as fast as we could and once almost overtook you, but the pirates following you were between us. They would have murdered us, and could have easily enough, but I called down such curses upon them that they were terrified. But we must go on again, for there is no safety on this island. Others will come after us."

Lasa and the two men unharnessed their spent horses and set them free. They doubled up with the others and in a minute or two the group was on its way again. There was no time for mother to embrace daughter or friend to greet friend. The chariots set off at as fast a pace as they could possibly maintain. Mile after mile passed beneath their horses' hoofs, and still they swept on, looking behind them at intervals to see if they were followed. Fortunately, no cloud of dust appeared. In the late afternoon they came to the coast.

Far out at sea a ship lay at anchor. If their luck still held, this would be their rescue ship. Quickly Yarem and the two boys lit fires. When the three fires were burning brightly, they tossed green leaves and grass on them and the resulting heavy smoke billowed upward in dark whirling columns. Those on the ship ought to be able to see the signals. At first nothing happened.

Finally the ship started beating in toward shore. They were going to be safe!

An hour later everyone was aboard. Rest and food and drink seemed unreal. They could not realize that they were not still racing along the dusty roads of Crete, fleeing for their lives. And even as they took their ease on deck, the steady beat of horses' hoofs seemed to thunder in their ears, and their eyes to smart from the dust. It was hard to think, hard to make a decision when their very bones cried out "Do nothing!"

Yarem, though, had thought of a new problem. "This is the time, I feel sure, to collect the treasure. We may not have another easier chance. As yet this is only an invasion, but if affairs continue as badly as they have started, there will soon be no Royal Navy to protect us. The pirates will be unrestrained, and who knows when we will be able to get back here again. So let us gather the treasure while we can and then make for Egypt."

This was good reasoning and everyone agreed to it. The ship moved on along the coast to the cove that gave access to the shrine. As the familiar shore line came into sight, Ar said to Yarem, "Nari knows how to reach the cliff entrance to the cave, so there is no need to go around to the shrine and betray our presence to anyone who might be nearby. We know the passage to the

160

storage chamber only too well; we have been over it and over it in the dark. With torches it will be easy. Besides, we left the trail of cord there; we did not roll it up. We can lower the treasure right down the cliff."

Yarem thought they could. He told the crew just what Ar had suggested and Nari was pleased to learn that she was to be the guide. They anchored in the cove, and soon Nari was scaling the cliff with a sailor behind her carrying a light rope. This was attached to a heavy rope ladder which he pulled up to the opening as soon as he reached it. Other sailors followed to help and in a few hours not a bale or chest or box remained in the great secret chamber. The last trip through the passage was made, everything had been taken down the cliff without accident, and all was ready for departure. Then they discovered that Nari was missing. She reappeared almost at once, however, with the rope ladder. "We couldn't leave that dangling," she said. "It would betray the hiding place. Who knows, we might want to use it again one day."

Pta said, "Good for you, Nari." After all, he was going home. He could afford to pay Nari a compliment, for without her he didn't know just where he would be now. And, he decided, he could forget about her prowess at wrestling. Ar hoped he would never see that cave again, but he, too, told Nari how clever she had been to think of the rope ladder. He was ashamed of himself for thinking it, but wasn't Nari almost too perfect? Now in Egypt, girls — Suddenly he thought of his sister and was homesick.

The oarsmen began pulling toward Egypt.

When at last the shores of his homeland came into view, Ar could hardly contain himself. Here he was returning from his first voyage and from his first battle. He was tense with excitement and tried to point out for the others sites he remembered as important historic spots. But the low-lying land afforded little in the way of landmarks and he discovered that he hadn't much to say, particularly since his feelings were so deep. What could one say about one's own country to weary strangers; how could one express what one felt? He looked appealingly at Yarem and realized at once that Yarem's own feelings were mixed. Yarem's experiences in Egypt had not been too pleasant.

Yarem smiled at Ar as though reading his mind and said, "Well, Ar, you have had some unpleasant adventures in my country, haven't you? So we are even. . . . I suppose you cannot wait to get to shore."

Indeed, Ar was ready, even to clutching the

bundle that contained his precious necklace. "There is just one thing," he said, looking at Yarem. "You and Mother Artish, Lasa and Nari will be guests in my home, so we will all be together — like one big family. But what about Ubi and Lysis?" He moved quickly toward Yarem as he spoke, stumbled over a coil of rope and dropped his bundle. The necklace spilled out and clattered to the deck. To his horror, he saw two of the emerald scarabs become detached and roll away. Ubi and Lysis were standing nearby and just in time, each of them scooped up a jewel before it rolled too close to the edge of the deck. As they brought the jewels back to Ar, who thanked them, Lasa appeared at his elbow. "It is an omen," she said. "You were just speaking about Ubi and Lysis?"

"Yes, we were," said Yarem. "Ar was wondering what will become of them now. He feels that they have been such loyal friends." Ubi and Lysis said nothing; they too were wondering what would happen to them in Egypt where their master had been treated so badly much of the time. But they did not change their expressions. They listened.

Lasa had drawn herself up into her priestess attitude and now spoke as if in a prophetic trance, but this time gently. Nari moved closer; her

163

mother was about to indicate things to come and Nari was curious. Lasa said, "The treasure is saved to be put to proper use. Be wise, my child, and give of your treasure to those who must go farther than we know."

Ar had come to know Lasa well enough by this time to know that whether she spoke with the voice of the Mother Goddess or with the voice of Lasa, she was right always and her advice should be taken. He thought a moment, then, with a great emerald scarab in each hand, he walked over to Ubi and Lysis and gave Ubi the scarab in his right hand and Lysis the scarab in his left hand. "There," he said. "You saved them from the sea and they are yours. May their goodness be eternal."

Emerald scarab from the Egyptian Necklace

"But your beautiful necklace," said Nari impulsively.

"Hush, Nari," Lasa reprimanded her. "Ar is right." Nari was ashamed of herself for what was perhaps the first time in her life and resolved to tell Ubi and Lysis so at the first opportunity. But now Ar was starting to wrap up his precious necklace again. Then he paused and held it out in front of him. The jewels and gold winked in the sun. Next, he placed it around his neck but did not fasten it. "See," he said, "is it not improved? Those two dangling scarabs rather spoiled the, the —"

Yarem finished the sentence for him. "The symmetry?" he suggested. "Yes," Ar agreed. "They were always a little in the way." He carefully wrapped up the necklace.

Lysis had considered for some time how to show his gratitude, then he spoke. "I thank you, Ar," he said, "more than I can say. But I prefer to think that whenever you see those two vacant places on the necklace, you will think of Ubi and me and what you have done for us. I have known you long enough to realize that the treasure you give away is of all things the most valuable to you. Speaking for myself, I hope that you will always remember what you have done today. May we be worthy of your gift."

165

Ubi expressed himself more simply. He just said, "Thank you," but his eyes glistened in his fine, dark face, and all those present knew that they spoke for him.

The moment had become much too meaningful. Everyone on deck was relieved when a shout from shore indicated that they were about to land — in Egypt! Ar wished that his father might have had business that would have brought him to this port at the Delta of the Nile — how splendid it would be if Het could meet them as they stepped ashore. But it was most unlikely, Ar realized, for how could Het have known of their arrival? Still, the rest of the journey up the river to Thebes would be nothing — then he would be home again!

So it was that two important links of the queen's necklace began their own journeys up and down the world, Ubi's scarab accompanying him still farther south toward his home in Africa, and the scarab Ar gave to Lysis heading north to the Greek mainland where Lysis was born.

MYRON TIM PALMER

MYRON TIM PALMER was born and brought up in Wauseon and Toledo, Ohio. He attended Toledo University but received his B.F.A. in painting from Syracuse University in New York and his M.A. in the practice of art from Oberlin College. He has taught in Ohio and Pennsylvania schools and is presently the art teacher at the Vernon L. Davey Junior High School in East Orange, New Jersey.

Mr. Palmer's avocations and hobbies include reading, history, gardening, and, of course, painting — his paintings have been included in several group and two one-man shows. *The Egyptian Necklace* and *Treachery in Crete* are his first two books.

These books, and the two set in Mycenae and Rome which will follow, were written because Mr. Palmer believed there were too few books for junior high school students about art history which would lead them to delve further into the study of ancient art. The author's main concern has been to keep the historic side of his books correct and to fit the fiction to it.